The Valley

a mystery novel by

Paul Riedel

www.paul-riedel.de

©Paul Riedel, Munich 2019

Printed in Germany

Cover: © Paul Riedel, Munich 2017

First German edition 2017
Second German edition 2018
First English edition 2019

Bibliographic information of the German national library: The German national library registered this publication in the German national bibliography, detailed bibliographic data are available online at www.dnb.de.

© 2018 Paul Riedel
Production and publisher
BoD- Books on Demand, Norderstedt

Paul Riedel

Paul Riedel is a name which is recurrent in my family for many generations. You could suppose this family is short on imagination when it comes to naming their new-borns; however you would be mistaken! It is a family where phantasy is handed down from one generation to another.

We had an art historian, an editor, a technical draftsman and now me, in the current generation as an artist and computer scientist in our family. This shows that all Paul Riedels stayed true to art, directly or indirectly. As I don't have any sons, this line of Pauls will end, as long as one of my sisters won't change my prophecy for a wonder. All of my ancestors had, besides their art, another career going.

I was born in Brazil where I grew up under a mixed upbringing which included knowing about mixed ethnicity. I was raised in an afro-brazilian family whobelieved and baptised me in Umbanda, the Brazilian pagan believe which originates in Africa. I experienced the strict, Italian Catholics. From my mother's side I learned about the Neapolitan, and Umbrian origin to the Lutheran origin came from my father. I developed a comprehensive vision of believe and reality.

Preamble

Revenge is the keynote which already lead to the death of many people. If thought about death as a remedy or the end to inflicted pain, it will only be after the death of someone's tormentor that they would realise, there is not a remedy to every sorrow.

There are many reasons to inflict pain. Abuse of power, ignorance or characteristic weaknesses are just a few examples.

People or animals who have to suffer from such pain are most of the time weaker and unprepared. They don't offer resistance. However, if they survive those tortures, they create their own values. Values which have nothing in common with money, power or ownership but just with their will to survive.

Many of these people are children who are equally as innocent as our pets which are just seeking for a life in harmony and love.

Quite often, the perpetrators of these painful experiences in the life of others believe in God. Allegedly, it is a God of mercy and love, of values of those who only seldomly believe in such kind of God.

But if you open your eyes up to see reality, you would realise that the alleged mercy and love of those Gods is just a lure for his victims. In a swirl of materialistic goods, the victims can give up, offer resistance or even give this materialistic world new order.

A few victims found this option and decided to fight to survive.

The Puppet

The first rays of sunshine, which came through the little window on the other side of the room, shone onto the dark wall. Angelika watched the sunlight creating shapes on the ingrained wallpaper and wondered how long she could still stay in this room. She stopped counting the days, but it had to be a few years already since she was narcotised and set foot in this room. "Set foot!" she thought. This phrase doesn't describe the situation very well.

She was carried into this room like an old sack of clothes, and now she was sure she would leave the room the same way she entered it. Dragged around and unconscious.

She pulled herself together to get up and pick up the breakfast, which was pushed through the narrow slot in the door. It will probably be one of those stone-like mixtures which should actually be jelly or the not identifiable pulp which they call a cereal. No matter which it will be, it would all taste the same, if it did taste like anything.

"No contact with the staff." This is what the responsible doctor, told her.

"She is confused and has to be protected from this environment before we can be successful with her therapy."

She never actually saw her doctor before. She could only remember how his voice echoed through the room and how all the assistants scribbled down notes and nodded in response to everything he said.

Angelika was only half-conscious because the sedatives they gave her were too potent for her. The following days did not get better, and everything was dulled by the medications they made her take. She even wet the bed sometimes because she just lost control over herself.

The assistant diagnosed her with "hebephrenia and dangerous paranoid occurrences" and noted it in her medical chart.

She was helpless when they rolled her into the room and threw her on her bed.

The sunlight got brighter, and she could identify a palm tree on the ingrained wallpaper.

The toilet was in the same room as her, which lead to the office smelling accordingly. She couldn't tell if it was the scent of cheap soap or old urine. It didn't happen very often that a nurse came into the room and even less regularly that someone actually cleaned her room. She had the choice of either cleaning the room herself or to live with the smell. A Greek guy of whom she could never recall his name came in every now and then and groped her. She felt embarrassed every time. He wasn't unattractive, but she felt like if she got dirtier every time he came in.

It was planned that today someone would come to clean her room. It would surely be the Greek guy. As this happens about once a month and it was about the fiftieth time someone actually cleaned her room, it was a good indication that she had been locked in this hole for about four years already.

"Angelika?", shouted a voice from the outside of the door.

She turned around in her bed, now facing the wall.

A little window in the door opened where two sharp eyes appeared.
"It's sunshining day." It was the Greek guy.

Angelika whined like a moody child and pulled her duvet over her head.

"My love. I don't want to sedate you again. You have to promise that you won't try to run out of the room or start screaming." The nurse sounded strict but gentle. However, although his voice might sound loving, it was threatening as well.

"Yes", Angelika whined.

"Get up. Take your breakfast and be a good girl. Can we agree on that?"

"Girl?" She thought despitefully. She was older than sixty, and the guy at the door looked like he only had his first shave yesterday.

"Yes", she whined again. This time it was a long and stretched Yes.

"I'll be back in half an hour with the cleaning material. Are you okay with this, darling?"

Angelika wished she was strong enough to hit the nurse with a brush so hard that he could never call her "love" or "darling" again. However, she knew, she didn't have the strength and talking back would only be a waste of time.

The palm tree at the wall now looked like a tiara and something similar to a horse, she thought.

Her mental state wasn't in the best condition anymore after spending so many years in this souterrain. Without seeing the sun once or any kind of human interaction, she lost every connection to reality.

"I'll be a good girl for you today. We'll have a lot of fun together."

She waited for a response which, as expected, came immediately.

"Naughty girl. I'll be back in a minute."

She jumped out of bed, and her whole body was aching because of the lack of exercise. But she survived ten days already without taking her medication and she kind of enjoyed the pain.

This time she was prepared for him to molest her again. She wouldn't offer resistance. This time she was ready to finally end her time in captivity.

There are always pedestrians running around in the valley of Munich. No matter if it is the weekend or during the week, they are busy exploring the city, going shopping or simply sitting in one of the local restaurants, enjoying a beer.

Many companies rent offices there, and the magnificent entrance halls or the high-quality refurbishment of the office floors indicate how famous these companies exactly are.

Looking through an antique wooden-framed window onto the tower of the Saint Peters Church on the Viktualienmarkt in Munich shows this is a rather posh part of the city.

The sun shone bright and relentlessly through the blinds which she just let down. It forced Anne to get up to shut them a bit further.

She played an alleged heavy-metal song, which almost sounded too calm and peaceful to be categorised as such, in the background while she chatted with her other virtual friends online.

Although Anne was not a groupie of this band, it was one of the reasons for her eclectic taste in music. Listening to this particular song was once part of some research she had to do.

Anne was already in her thirties but looked, thanks to mother nature, still like she was seventeen. Many were surprised when they found out her actual age. Some even thought, she faked her ID.

While she pressed the button on the wall to correct the positioning of the blinds, she received more messages from other chat members.

Her right hand showed signs of abuse which she had to go through a few years ago. During her work as a hacker, she stepped on someone's toes a bit too much. This unfortunate encounter left her with scars on her right hand and a missing pinkie finger. She no longer missed the lost finger while typing on her keyboard.

However, in some bad moments when she looked down on her hand, all the memories came back of how she sat in a dark and dusty basement in Switzerland. Being tied to a chair, she was beaten hard and had to beg for her life.

A memory of the emerald ring of a lawyer on the ring finger of whoever hit her on her right cheek was carved into her mind like marble. The small scar on the corner of her eye made sure she would not forget this day although she got lucky in the last minute.

'It's already the third dog which came to an end like this. This man is a monster.' This post popped up showing the avatar of ALize, who wrote this statement.

The blinds crunched on and had a hard time turning the blades.

For a short time, Anne massaged the point where she lost her finger. Sometimes, she had a few cramps at this spot.

'I always knew it will be a person eventually.' BetaMoron undermined her statement with a crying Emoji.

The message, which summoned this online circle, was the confirmation of the suicide of a woman in Wolfratshausen. Her depression eventually ended her life for her.

Finally, the blinds were in the right position. Anne's finger hurt a bit because of the restive knob.

'Franzi's depression got bad since Basco got shot, she did nothing but crying all day long. We chatted a few times.' ALize probably worked out more than there actually was about this virtual friendship, but at least

she was the only one who felt like contradicting this statement.

A few thumbs-ups, crying Emojis or Emojis with a sad face were proof that many people read the post and expressed their sympathy.

Anne dropped a request in another window and found out that there actually were more than five-hundred messages between Franzi and ALize. This evaluation did not state whether the statements matched or if the response actually considered the alleged friend but apparently, their paths actually crossed. Anne looked up the IP address of both participants and could confirm again that they did talk to each other.

'ALize, who will look after her little puppy now?', asked BetaMoron.

'I think it is with a friend. I didn't read anything about it actually.'

In this chat forum, Anne's pseudonym was Fanny. Every day, she created new profiles online in different chats and on social media sides to get information about what happens worldwide.

'But Basco was old. Which puppy are you talking about, Beta?' Anne wanted to find out more as she didn't know this part of the story.

'The perpetrator or his friends bought a puppy for her as a replacement for Basco. The problem is, you can replace things, but not trust and confidence', stated BetaMoron. The term confidant is mostly used in the Dragons and Dungeons game but not really for animals, which are attached to its master mentally. Anne assumed that BetaMoron was a role-player. In another window on her desktop, she looked up the name BetaMoron and immediately found it where she thought it would be.

'But how sure can you actually be that the hunter shot the dog deliberately?', interfered Anne again. Her avatar was a pink unicorn with blue wings. *'In her suicide note, Franzi stated his name. Apparently, she already blamed him for animal cruelty before, but no one ever did anything.'* BetaMoron seemed really invested in this topic. She also posted a link which leads to Franzi's suicide note. She uploaded this letter shortly before her death to her profile.

A picture of the hunter next to the head of the police of this district indicated his great relationship to the municipality and the local politicians.

'He's probably caudate with an inferiority complex who lets it out on those poor animals.' ALize was not very sensitive when picking her words. Her avatar was a pirate with a raised sword, which put further pressure on the conversation. In yet another window, Anne looked up animal abuse in this district. She wasn't overly surprised to find more than a thousand hits on this topic. She refined her search and set a date to make sure the emotions in this chat didn't mix up with weird statements of some trolls. There were still more than three hundred cases. She searched for reoccurring terms and found that Peter-Anton, as well as the hunting association "Holy Hubertus" came up frequently.

The song in the background came to an end. The next one had more bass and the high-pitched voice of a girl who apparently reached maturity.

'How old was Franzi?', asked Anne's avatar.

'Her neighbour released a death notice. Click on this link here.' BetaMoron attached a link to her message. Anne clicked on it, and the picture of a sixty-year-old woman appeared. She stood next to a golden retriever which apparently died shortly before her.

'They are reunited now', stated Anne together with a crying Emoji.

'I will get my ass off of my chair and drive over to the funeral. It will be in the village next to mine, and I have nothing else to do. I have to protest against this prick.', ALize posted a sticker of a banana shaking her ass to make her statement a little bit funnier.

'I didn't know Franzi, but I will post an E-card on her profile.'

'Beta, you can do something as well and send a sympathy card to the funeral, and yes, you did know Franzi as well. We talked a few times about the campaign against halal meat on 'Freunden-Haus'', ALize seemed very determining. 'Freunden-Haus' is the name of a chatroom for people from the area who talk about local matters.

'Oh, her, yes. You are right.'

'I can't come. It's too far away for me', lied Anne, as always. Sometimes, she couldn't determine what reality was and what's not, and because she had so many different avatars and invented so many stories, she even dreamt about other personalities. Just one thing helped her keeping her true identity.

The blue unicorn with its pink wings, which she always selected as her profile picture.

'I could kill myself', said ALize.

'I have to go back to work', Anne responded and ended it as always with 'CU', signalising that she would be back soon. Usually that's not the case.

As always, Anne deleted her profile with the name Fanny and started the process of creating a new one. During this process, she inspected the incident she just discussed with the others in the chatroom.

Apparently, Peter-Anton was a cruel guy who killed a dog named Basco out of revenge. The owner suffered severe depression after that and poisoned herself with pills which lead to her death. A neighbour found her dead body one day later.

'A sad case, just like many others in this world where cruel things happen every day', she thought.

On her desktop, she had a few neatly organised folders, and one of those folders was named Peter-Anton. She put the protocols of chats which she visited and some documents she found online in this folder. Anne was very fussy about putting pictures, news clippings and other links in an organised order. Everything had to be ordered by date as well.

Earlier cases of animal cruelty were marked on a card which also showed potential connections to the hunter's association of Peter-Anton. She drew circles around the area where he lived and where this association was based.

The door of her office stood slightly ajar before it was opened completely, and a small man walked straight through it.

"Do you have anything new?" Gutto, the scene builder of the model agency "The Valley" came into her office.

"Damn. One day you'll kill me." Anne was obviously shocked by Gutto's sudden appearance. The music in the background drowned almost every other noise close to the office.

"Did you watch online porn? Naughty girl", Gutto laughed about scaring Anne. His half-closed eyes should emphasise his predatory assumption.

Anne put her hair up today. Her black curls with red highlights were placed on top of each other elegantly. It reminded a little bit of a statue of a fury.

"Only perverted men like you and your husband would do that. I'm looking for details about a suicide and the poor dog which was killed in Wolfratshausen."

Anne couldn't stand animal cruelty and hunters, but Gutto became actually furious every time.

"I hate hunters. They claim to help the environment although they actually destroy it."

"This here is a special case. Cruelty is just one part of how he harms our environment.

Gutto was a small man who looked friendly even when he was actually furious.

"I wanted to send the file over to you and your husband."

"Not now, please, my love. We are still busy with the Honourable Sophie and a fashion show in Frankfurt. And you know, you shouldn't edit pictures and create the perfect stage scenery for a fashion show while you have coffee and cake. We'll be free next week. I also have to work as a car mechanic, and I have to get this done today." Gutto left the room, and his small hands waved like butterflies, looking like he wanted to fly away.

"Drama Queen," Anne ended the conversation.

"Mechano Queen, please!" Gutto disappeared around the corner.

The phone was ringing.

"Hi," Anne answered the phone.

She nodded twice and turned down the music in the background.

"I received a message that Eleonore will go to the hospital?" Paloma, lawyer of the agency, asked.

"Yes, Paloma. Eleonore will go into a new hospital in two weeks again."

"Again? She should enjoy a holiday instead!"

Anne nodded.

"I'm not sure if she knows what she's doing. But who could find out? She is crazy."

Paloma knew this undertone in Anne's voice very well.

"Is your depression back?"

"Not worse than usual. The new case brings back unlucky memories, but it'll be better soon." Anne paused. "I think."

"In case you need an ear to listen, I have one left." Both laughed. Paloma was deaf on one ear. When she was young, she was abused by her mother. She lost her ability to hear after an unlucky slap in her face.

"You're silly", teased Anne.

"What case are you working on?"

"Suicide of the woman in Wolfrathshausen. I thought she would push through a bit longer. I didn't see this coming."

"It is not your fault. No one here is a psychic."

"Gutto is planning on tinkering cars, he just told me."

"Gutto? I wouldn't like driving that car." Paloma laughed, which didn't happen very often.

"I think nobody would be keen on driving a car, knowing Gutto worked on it. See you later."

Anne put the phone down and opened up her new profile on her desktop. Her original name was AliciaKee.

That's how a new conversation started with a forced prostitute from Brazil who currently sat in an internet café in Frankfurt.

"I just read that you are scared of getting beaten up. For real?"

All of this happened a few months earlier, but only a year later Peter-Anton's story took an unexpected turn for him.

Ballerina

Telling a story after everything is over can be very easy because of how distance it might seem and because problems were already solved in the past. Eleonore had to fight her memories, which sometimes seemed so far away.

Although some details might get lost over time, an experience leaves marks so profoundly, they are seemingly unforgettable. This was exactly how Eleonore saw the world, right before she fell asleep.

Eleonore was trapped in her mind and memories and thought about how she could explain her incident to her therapist in the upcoming session.

She tried to start off with the part of her life during which she actually lived. As a young girl, she was never as cool as she wished she would be. She had to live with disappointments, which later turned out just to be of puberty. Back then, drama and intrigues were perceived as more emotional than what she learned in her later life. Those thoughts made the imagination of the upcoming session with her therapist a bit more concrete.

When she was sixteen, she already knew that she would never become a supermodel. She gained too many curves around her hips, a trait she definitely inherited from her mother. The pale skin was definitely from her father and this mixture, combined with the bad taste in fashion and make-up of her favourite aunt, wasn't the best, according to some fellow students.

She wasn't sure if she should mention this to her therapist.

"No", she answered the question that was on her mind in an undertone.

This was the reason why she didn't care too much about boys as well. She tried to avoid rejections and immature apologies after cancelled dates. The men who looked at her, despite all those disadvantages, didn't seem to realise her femininity. And if they did, they were old, disgusting or dodgy and only prompted the feeling of wanting a shower rather than any kind of passion.

Most of the time, women only liked her if she sewed or cooked for them. Her family had a fine tradition in needlework and Eleonore spent many hours designing new clothes. They were a replacement for her dolls, and her dolls were the models. That is how it had been her whole life.

It is essential to mention the "school-break lesbians". That's how the owners of the café were called to which a few girls, including Eleonore, went during her lunch break. Both of them were very friendly and always had an eye out for "new members" as malicious people gossiped. Eleonore though they were really lovely, but only as acquaintances. Their friendship consisted only of saying hi to each other during lunch breaks. The two owners of the café were barely aware of their reputation. With the rental prices of the city they had other problems on their minds. This made Eleonore realise that all of the other rumours were most likely a creation of someone's fantasy and not based on actual reality.

"We better let it be." She talked to herself again and quickly stopped thinking about this as she found it to be too personal.

Eleonore didn't have many friends; therefore she tried to find work as soon as possible to fulfil her dream of eventually finding the love of her life.

Caught in her thoughts, she pulled her duvet over her shoulders and continued to think about a time in her past. She didn't dream at all that night.

◆

"Hello, darling!", the Greek guy welcomed her.

Angelika's mental illness transformed her into a mixture of an innocent and cruel type of girl. Despite her age, mentally, she could still be kind of immature. Her illness hebephrenia was named after the clumsy goddess Hebe, who spilt the Ambrosia on the table of Gods. As a punishment, she was replaced as a cupbearer by the youngest admirer of Zeus, Ganymed.

"Haaii!", replied Angelika in one, long syllable which sounded like it would never end.

"You are tame today. That's nice. I just clean your room, and then we can play with each other", said the Greek guy while he pulled a cleaning bucket together with a brush into her room.

She knew how this would go off. She thought about the exact process for a few days now.

He quickly went outside in the hallway and looked for someone behind him or within earshot. Angelika knew what he was planning on doing. She memorised every one of his exact steps during the last months. He acted almost like a robot, which reeled off the same program every time.

Angelika got out two balls of strings from under her pillow. She formed those out of old strings of her clothes. She threw them discretely under her bed, right towards the wall.

"There are ugly dust bunnies under the bed", she sulked. Quickly she pulled up her dress to briefly blow her nose.

"All of those will be gone by the time I'm finished." He paused and locked the door. He put the keychain in his pocket.

Angelika's eyes followed the keys like a hunting lynx.

The Greek guy cleaned the only table in the room. Apart from that, there was only the bed and a chair for visitors, which was used very seldomly. In the back part of the room was only the toilet and an awkward shower which was already mouldy.

Two screws were rolling on the floor. The Greek guy pushed them around with his dust mop. He looked and threw them, without even thinking about it, into the rubbish bag, which was on the cleaning trolley.

"The toilet stinks." Angelika frowned her nose to emphasise her statement and to show that she couldn't help herself. With those comments, she could distract the cleaner from touching her again.

"Do you like it now?", he asked extra friendly to create some friction between them. He wanted to establish trust, so he could get in the mood for what he was about to do, and she wouldn't offer much resistance.

"Do you want one of the pink pills?" he asked. Those sedatives made her totally submissive, and most of the time she slept the whole day after taking one of them.

"Noooo" The Greek guy knew that a No as long as this could end his whole game before it even started. That's why he left the pill in his pocket.

"Do you want to play with me today?", he asked while he quickly cleaned the floor with his wet mop.

"Yeeees!" Angelika was looking under her mattress for something, and the Greek guy thought it would be her rag doll.

"Did you lose Gazou?"

"No. He sits at the window." Angelika showed him by pointing her finger in the direction of the window while she pulled back her dress with her other hand.

This was the first time she said yes to him without being so resistant. He was happy. He quickly went to the door and made sure no one was around. Most of the other employees were on holiday. There was only one colleague downstairs at the sanatorium, and he usually made him go food shopping.

"Ahh. You're so nice. We'll have a lot of fun together with Gazou."

"Yeees", she replied and pulled her dress up a bit higher. She knew that he liked her despite her age. He probably doesn't find a woman very often who can stand his smell.

He realised that she rubbed something off of the wall. The floor seemed to be sanded by something at this part.

He quickly finished mopping the room and lastly cleaned the sink and the toilet with a cloth.

"Lay in bed. I will be with you soon."

"But there are still the dust bunnies."

"I cleaned them all away."

"No. I can see them. You have to chase them away with your hands."

He hesitated for a second but went on his knees and cleaned under her bed. He realised parts of her bed frame were loose. That's probably where the screws came from. The bed was already a few years old. He always knew that they had to change it eventually.

"We have to fix your bed."

He found another two dust bunnies far under her bed. They looked like Angelika made them herself and threw them under her bed. He thought she might be into playing hide and seek.

"I found the dust bunnies."

"Ahh."

"There you go. They are all gone now", he was still under her bed. He leaned onto the bed while getting up, and he didn't even know what happened, but he suddenly felt a metallic coldness all the way down his throat into the direction of his stomach, and the taste of iron filled his mouth.

That's when she realized that the missing part of the bed was now bored into him. One last thought made him clear that the sanded part of the floor was what she used as a grindstone.

Quick fingers were looking for the keys in his pocket. He wanted to call for help, but Angela gagged him with one of her old panties.

Angelika picked up Gazou off of the windowsill and all the medications which she didn't take over the last twenty days fell onto the wet floor.

The Greek guy realised he underestimated Angelika. What a tragic mistake.

He lost his conscience and only heard how Angelika closed the door behind her. He never woke up again.

On a sunny day in March, Eleonore woke up after a good night's rest. The sun forced its way through a slit in her heavy purple curtains. She didn't close the blinds in front of the big window. They were only part of the decorations of the big farmer's house, which was built in the middle of an extensive area.

It was like many mornings before. She had to stare at the white ceiling and think about what she had to do on this day. She remembered that she had a meeting with her therapist at eleven o'clock today.

Her migraine was worse than usual today. That's something that can be expected in the most southern state of Germany, the Free State of Bavaria. Bavaria is a beautiful country, blessed with the Alps and a warm climate. However, the prettier the colour of the sky, the heavier the foehn effect. This warm and see-through cloud dips the sky in a dark blue, which made them looked like out of a painting.

A quick look on the clock radio to her left on the nightstand showed that she slept longer than she actually wanted to. Her bedroom was precisely how someone would imagine a typical girly room out of the eighties. Although the Biedermeier furniture showed that the family wasn't poor, the posters of rock musicians, which covered the walls, showed what kind of type the landlady was.

She looked at the wrinkly corners and colour spots and thought that those posters probably had better days in the past.

Her clothes were all neatly on top of a chair, but she didn't know where her shoes are. She realised that her clothes are a bit too neatly for how she would've put them there.

Her make-up, which was a collection of every kind of quality, was piled up on a tray, just like at a sale of a flea market. She looked at it and thought of her aunt.

She didn't have any perfumes, and if she did, she probably wouldn't find any of them shortly. One more time, she looked from the window to the ceiling. It was hard for her to push the heavy duvet aside.

Right next to the bedroom door was, behind an open door, the small bathroom. The brown tiles glared slightly in the scarce light, which shone through the ventilation in the ceiling. She looked back to the clock and realised that it was already one hour ago when she decided to get up. She jumped out of bed like a cat and went quickly into the bathroom. The smell under her armpits indicated that she didn't spend enough time in there. The result didn't look quite as good as what she had hoped for, and she couldn't find one mirror which wasn't packed with clothes and cloths, so she had to brush her hair back quickly. She hoped her appearance had approved accordingly.

As always, her breakfast stood already fully prepared on the table at the other window. Most of the time she slept so deep, she only seldomly noticed the service coming in her room. She didn't really care because she never spoke one word to her and didn't expect to change that. She had too many things on her mind to focus on gossiping as well. Eleonore just knew she didn't want to miss any details while talking to her therapist. Today was supposed to be the last meeting with him, so she had to make sure everything was sorted correctly.

She dried her legs with a towel and realised that her skin feels unpleasantly dry. She thought she might need to buy another body lotion. Eleonore went through her clothes and smelled all of them, looking for something clean, or at least something that felt like it was.

She looked through the window and saw a car parked up the driveway. That's how she knew that she'd be running late for her appointment.

By accident, she chose the panties with the burst elastic band, and now they were sliding down her thigh, which was a bit too thin for her figure. Apparently, the elastic band was a bit too old. She pulled it up again, now almost annoyed, tied a knot at the side and made sure the blue dress she picked was straight again.

Never would she throw away a pair of underwear so expensive, so she knew, sooner or later, she had to sew it.

Eleonore quickly looked at herself in the window and tried to find out if she looked attractive or not.

"Details, details." She threw her hands in the air and ran back to her wardrobe where she picked up a brooch in the form of a blue unicorn out of her drawer. She attached it on the left side of her dress. This little something, she got from her friend should make her feel like she's not alone.

Eleonore wasn't satisfied with how she looked, but it was all she could do today. She opened the door leading out to the balcony and carried the breakfast, which the service left in her room, outside. Initially, she wasn't planning on inviting Richard, her therapist, for breakfast but now that is was so late already, she didn't have another option.

The nameless service must have thought so as well as she put out a second table setting on the balcony already. It made Eleonore believe that maybe the service knew her better than she thought.

She heard a car driving through the entrance gate. It had to be the delivery man of the kitchen. She tried to quickly clean up her room, threw a few pieces of clothing into the washing basket and hung up the curtains.

It was another lovely day in the outskirts of Munich.

◊

She felt the pain in her feet, and the floor was cold, but she couldn't go back anymore.

At the end of the hallway was a door leading out onto the yard. Angelika knew it was open because the Greek guy liked to air this room on the days when he was cleaning.

She went from the door straight to the bush behind the apple trees. She could remember that the river wasn't far from there.

Angelika had to remember those better days when she founded this hospital together with her husband. She knew she was ill, but she was also aware that the reason for her illness had to end eventually.

Dry twigs broke where she walked, and thorns poked her smooth skin.

"There's no time for pain or complaining." Angelika talked to Gazou, the ragdoll which stared through its glass eyes into nothing.

The wind was wet and cold while she was walking down the hill.

She remembered opening this hospital for bored, rich women. She was rich, and her husband was young and handsome, but unfortunately not very intelligent. In the summers, he walked around the swimming pool in a super short thong and strutted with this firm bit of fabric in front of women who longed for him and envied Angela.

"The round of fitness will begin in a bit my dears, please go to the exercise room," she heard herself announcing the training.

Those years were wonderful, they were apart of joy filled with enemies and haters.

The last day before the start of her trauma rewinds in her head every day.

"I hope I'll be as pretty as you are eventually. I just can't lose weight", cried Nancy, one of her clients.

"Don't be unthankful. Those ten years of cake and fats of all them dumplings surely can't vanish within then days." Both women laughed.

"Angelika," shouted an assistant.

"Yes. What's up?" The assistant pulled Angelika aside and smiled at Nancy, who now realised the conversation wasn't meant for her ears.

"Some men came who claim to be the new members of this institute."

"Excuse me?"

"Yes, and one of them wanted to see the accounts."

A surge of emotion went through her body, and she felt dizzy for a moment.

"Where are they?"

"In your office."

"Tell Eva she should do the Callanetics lessons. I'll look after them."

Her first thought was that her husband just did something without asking her for permission, and she had to pay for it now.

She got interrupted by a twig which fully hit her on the cheek while walking through the shrubs.

Then she spotted the lake further down in the valley.

"Let's go Gazou. We want to go swimming."

"Good morning, Leo!" That's how Richard called her, and as always, he emphasised his greeting with a smile. As usual, Eleonore was besotted by his nature and just never had the heart to tell him to knock before coming in. It was this moment when she remembered that she doesn't actually like her own name. Eleonore was the name of her aunt who she loved so much. Every girl of her generation had stylish names like Krissi, Jessy, Lyvi – that's why she preferred Leo to Eleonore.

Richard wasn't tall, and the fact that his stomach was quite round was too Bavarian for Eleonore's taste. Most of the time he was dressed as grey as his hair was. However, today he broke through this pattern by wearing a purple tartan scarf.

"I will bring our breakfast outside onto the balcony." She spoke like someone out of a detergent advertisement and laughed while swinging her non-existent trail. The flower pattern on her cotton dress tried to move, but the old, over-washed fabric didn't swing very well.

Richard came running to help her. His legs didn't help him to walk, but he kept his balance. His disability was never an issue for her. He had bandy legs, but he could walk more elegant than many other men Eleonore knew.

"The service only brought orange juice", complained Eleonore. She seemed disappointed.

"Well, I don't drink orange juice, my dear." His smile was as irresistible as always, and for a quick second Eleonore forgot what her plan was.

They positioned plates and cutlery neatly around the white cast-iron table. The cool glass plate was almost a bit too cold for her liking. The chair cushions were out on the chairs and ready to host their guests. As always, Richard was dressed very decently. Apart from his purple scarf, he could definitely not be described as a dandy. Eleonore had to bite her lip every time as she never managed to look as harmonic in the mornings as he does. Finely brushed hair and the smell of pines graced a tanned man who looked like a figure out of a picture of El Greco, the Greek artist from the Middle Ages.

Eleonore wasn't really awake yet and remembered only slowly that Richard was here with her to have one of their sessions.

She went through her memories and tried to mentally organise the logistics of what happened over and over again. However, she had to make peace with the fact that she just wasn't too good at telling her stories. She didn't know how often they sat on this balcony already when she wanted to pull her plan though, but every time she didn't succeed, and they ended the sessions on another topic.

"This is our last session, isn't it?" Eleonore asked to be completely sure.

"I think so. As far as I know, you are prepared perfectly."

"Did you know this place was a beauty clinic before?"

"Yes, I've known this house for a very long time."

"How long did you know this house?"

"Long. But I don't recall for how long. But let's not digress, we are here to talk about what you remember."

"I feel better when I imagine women went to this place worrying about their appearance and not about their mental state."

Richard nodded and tried to keep his looks from Eleonore's thin legs.

She was convinced the story started a while ago, and she was sure that starting at the beginning would help her explaining what had happened. She had to think, she would have cleaned up the table like this already and that everything that happened here, happened already. Just like a Deja-vu. Admittedly, this must have been the repercussions of the drinks of the night before. She wanted to avoid asking if they had something to drink, but she knew that whatever she had the night before, it was too much.

"I hope, this time I can manage to tell you what actually happened", started Eleonore with an insecure voice. She poured some coffee in one of the cups, and her eyes lingered on the liquid running out of the pot.

"We're not in a rush. I don't have anything else to do today, and as I promised, I will spend the morning with you. Tomorrow I will hand in my report to your boss." Richard smiled and, despite the bits of toast on his upper lip, he looked charming. Maybe even more than usual, she thought.

"I will start where reality and fantasy cross in my mind. I start with the story of the woman who never existed."

Eleonore coughed twice already and started over telling her story three times. Richard interpreted her hesitation as a sign of an internal fight between imagination, the reality, and what she thinks is reality. This was normal for a therapist and Richard prepared himself to be patient and rational. Every time she interrupted her story with another activity at the breakfast table. Typically, women started digging in their handbags and men crossed their legs. There are many signs of someone feeling uncomfortable before overcoming an obstacle.

"I can only tell you what someone told me, or at least what I think someone told me. Eventually, what I experienced or what I think I experienced. Please don't think I am crazy, but I think I understood the situation in some kind of way." Eleonore paused and got out a red fleece blanked which she stretched out over her legs. She also threw a wool scarf, which she brought out with her onto the balcony, over her shoulders. Her words sounded like apologies and although they didn't contain any kind of content, Richard listened patiently.

"Don't worry. I am not here to evaluate your story or its content. However, you need to verbalize what brought you here and how you perceive this story or reality. Tell me, and we will evaluate it together after I heard everything. Would that be fine for you?"

Eleonore still fought with the scarf, which tangled in a dry plant hanging from the wall. She put down her cup.

"I've been with "The Valley" for two years now. One of my tasks is to work at the reception and helping out with some things for the people there."

Richard nodded approvingly and noticed she started her story for the fourth time.

We prepared our summer exhibition in Munich, where we should host international guests this year. It was all about fashion not having any borders.

Eleonore waved her hand in a bow over her head to picture it more vividly.

"We invited two men from Morocco to a fashion show in Munich. Both of them could hardly believe their luck and said we would have made a mistake as none of them ever did anything with fashion. The call for bids was published on a French blog where they applied with their Selfies. The campaign was called "I'm so cool', and entertainers all over the world were asked to apply.

Richard nodded and got himself another fleece blanket out of the window box on the balcony to cover his legs. The cool wind was as refreshing as it was exhilarating.

"They were notified by a Social Media Network about this campaign. They presented themselves as 'Le charme marocain' and 'Moroccan Boyz', two DJs from El Jadida, Morocco. I've never been to a country like that for my holidays, but according to their application photos, this beach experienced some good days already. It was one of the beaches where families go to with their children and let them play the whole day until they fall into their beds at night, while their parents get drunk.

When Eleonore realised Richard seemed a bit absent, she coughed with emphasis to regain his attention.

Richard thought he saw something in the picture Eleonore painted in his mind. He remembered a family with two girls at the beach. The mother shouted: "Ahoy, pirates!" and the three of them went into the water. His memories were interrupted by a renewed cough.

"Don't worry, my dear. I can hear you. I just want to paint a picture in my head."

"Well, okay. Anne, who was the computer expert in the agency, located both the men and contacted them. They were excited and surprised. On the invitation, which they received via Email, was Sophie, our actually oldest model. Sophie must be taller than 1,80 m, and she has beautiful hair. I can't tell you the colour though, it's different on every picture. I think she's wearing wigs, but they don't look cheap." Eleonore emphasised this in a chatty undertone.

Richard signalised her with his hand that this is rather unimportant information and that she should move on.

"The show was supposed to be one month later. It was the time of Ramadan as well, and it seemed like in Plage d'el Jadida, the place where the two were from, was nothing on, so both DJs decided to go on this trip. As Anne said, she was sure that they could never decline this invitation."

Eleonore stared for a bit into nowhere and was caught in her thoughts. A wind made her talk faster as it seemed to be colder now.

"I picked them up a few days after they received the invitation. This was three days before the fashion show. I had to work extra hard because apparently, no one wanted to trust me with this responsibility."

"You own a car?" asked Richard, slightly surprised.

"No. The car was owned by the agency. A limousine. I'm not a good driver, but I can manage the way to the airport and back." Both of them laughed for a second after Eleonore imitated driving a car.

"Well, everything seemed normal until now, doesn't it?"

"Sure. Reality always seems very clear in the beginning, am I right?"

Richard didn't feel too comfortable with this statement. His eyes were twitching slightly, and he assumed Eleonore was looking for words which didn't want to come to her.

"Both men looked like they weren't used to women driving or being looked after by a woman who wasn't a prostitute. But I could live with that. Sure, the way they looked at me wasn't too pleasant but nothing I couldn't handle. Every two minutes, they had to organise their genitals in their trousers. Maybe they thought that'd make them even more irresistible. As far as I heard from female colleagues from Morocco, people weren't as traditional and old-fashioned as in other Muslim countries. They told me men behaved very much like machos. Not a holiday destination for women and homosexuals, right?" Eleonore laughed disapprovingly.

Richard nodded hesitantly after she mentioned his sexuality and gave her less feedback than she hoped she'd get. During this conversation, he kept a professional distance.

"On the next day, I was supposed to drive them to the city and show them where the fashion show will be. I was also instructed to show them the devices we would be using. I admit, I urged my boss to let me do it because I needed some fresh air and I wanted to do something nice for the two of them and me. I have to say, I soon realised that I'm more skilled with all the DJ equipment than both of them guys together. They were more like the men who get all the girls at parties, but definitely no DJs. I spent more than two hours instructing them. I did everything that was within my ability to speak French. I explained how to get the songs on the computer and that we don't have any record players, and that we didn't need them either. But I wasn't successful.

Eleonore signalised by lifting up her hands how helpless she was in this situation.

"They just didn't get it. They then started writing something and asked me a few questions. I drove them to a restaurant and tried to explain to them that we don't serve Halal and that I definitely don't support the consumption of it anyways."

Richard looked quite surprised.

"I'm fighting for animal rights. Fighting for the lives of animals and against the cruelty of humans. Horrible that we came that far in our evolution that people have to spy on other people now."

She shook her head and looked devastated. She poured some tea in hers and Richard's cup.

The tea smelled like herbs and flowers. It was unusual, and Richard tried to identify its taste.

"Is something up?", asked Eleonore.

"No. Please, just continue."

"I approached Anne, explained the situation with those two men and asked for advice. I was convinced those two weren't the DJs we needed for our show. Also, I really had to ask myself why they were here in the first place!"

Richard nodded and wrote something down.

"Apparently, Sophie just wanted them here, no matter how talented they were. Well, I was just there to do my job. Then, after everyone knew both of them were useless, we just left them in Munich overnight. I think they only stayed in the hotel the first night because they were tired from their journey. According to some statements, they've never flown before."

Eleonore had to laugh because she just couldn't believe there was anyone who was never on a plane before.

"Please, don't think I am looking down on them, but they were just too primitive for me."

Richard quickly rolled his eyes and tried to hide his judgment under the coat of professionalism.

"I never accompanied them to the hotel, I left them in front of it. Oh, and, a tall woman picked both of them up on their first day. In the mirrors of the car I saw how she even carried their heavy suitcases. After that, I had enough to do dealing with city traffic, and I couldn't see anymore." She waved her hands through the air and emphasised her statement.

Richard didn't miss to notice that it wasn't really likely and maybe a bit inappropriate to have a woman as a bellboy in Germany, but he didn't say anything.

"So, I was quite shocked about this selection of international guests, and I had to chat with Anne in the office. She knows everything about everyone in the office."

Eleonore squinted her eyes to try and look very perceptive. Then she seemed slightly insecure, and Richard wanted to cheer her up.

"What happened after that? What was your problem with such a normal situation? Everything seems very normal to me."

Eleonore lifted her hand as if she'd ask for a break. But then, she continued.

"Anne didn't want to comment on the reasons why those men got an invitation. But I am not stupid, I knew what had to be the reason."

"So?"

"Although Anne is a pro, I know my way around the internet as well, and I found their profiles and the pictures which they published before. I looked at their profiles and couldn't see anything out of the ordinary. Nothing useful at all. They just looked like gigolos and idiots who posed next to female tourists. Not the sort of men you want to be seen with. I have to say I can find everything online. Probably not as good as Anne, but almost as good."

It got a bit more exciting, and Eleonore was satisfied with this tagline and the role of a computer expert, which she gave herself.

"They had several pictures posing next to women, and I knew that this type of men wasn't suitable for our agency. Machos, homophobes with dodgy relationships to marginalised groups which aren't open to the rights women have in our world."

Richard understood that Eleonore was talking about radical believers who you hear a lot of on the news.

"Because there was nothing more to find, I had to stick to the plan. The two guys were supposed to meet Sophie in the evening. By the way, she wants to be called the Honourable Sophie, at least that is what I've been told. That woman has a thing for titles and wants to be approached like an aristocrat. Weird, is what I say. I think she can be a lot of work. I told you I never talked to her before, didn't I?"

"Numerous times since our first meeting. I wrote it down as well. How do you know what she wanted to be called?"

"Good question …" She paused and thought about this for a moment.

"I don't know. Wasn't important apparently, but I think Arnaud the photographer must have told me as he showed me his pictures once."

Both had to laugh about this chitchat and Eleonore imitated the Honourable Sophie.

"I picked up both of them dummies and brought them to the 'Inferno', which is a new night club on the Sonnenstraße in Munich. I parked exactly where dropped them off and indirectly signalised them to come towards me. I wasn't a fan of the situation, nor their behaviour."

She nodded a lot to stress her disgust.

Richard apparently didn't know this club. For several years now, the Sonnenstraße was known for having the most average shops in town. It wasn't top quality, but enough for those two visitors.

"It's the best you can get in this scene right now. Whoever works in the fashion industry needs to be seen once a month in another outfit in there. It's not the highest quality, but it's what is most popular. Ellen, Don Carmucci, Celso de Paula."

Eleonore waved some air towards herself while she took a sip of her tea. Richard didn't know any of those designer names. He never heard of them as he buys his clothes from the discounter or in a supermarket most of the time.

"You can imagine how shocked those men were. They were especially excited because of the boobs and all the women at the club. All those lights, all those people and sure, all the money those people spend in one evening. It was more than both of them could ever earn in a year, working as DJs on a beach."

Richard wrote down that until now, everything seemed reasonable for a life as a receptionist.

"I am sure we went to 'Inferno' together. I was looking for Sophie, and as I couldn't find her immediately, I asked the boss of the bar for the table of our agency, which I booked myself.

Several times, I saw pictures of Sophie in our agency, so I was sure I'd find her immediately.

We sat down at a table at the corner of the dance floor. I had to realise that this kind of dancing looked embarrassing to me. No proper steps, no choreography. Just a wild bouncing.

Well, I ordered a Rusty Nails for me as I needed something a little bit stronger to endure the night longer. I ordered in French."

She laughed and perfectly finished her presentation as a Grande woman.

"As I told you before, I think I've only seen pictures of Sophie until this day."

Richard nodded tiredly as he heard just this statement several timesduring this session. This was the fourth time he met up with Eleonore, and he was relieved that it'd be the last time. He was looking forward to handing in his report and finishing off this case.

Furthermore, he had to notice growing fatigue which made him assume that he would catch a cold or something worse soon.

"Even one hour later, no one showed up, and I was annoyed already. Especially because tomorrow was the fashion show and I had to perform as the new DJ as the two guys would never be able to work with our equipment."

The gardener started making unpleasant noise with his leaf blower. Richard went to the railing and shouted towards the gardener.

"Stop! Immediately. We are working here." Richard sounded like he would own the house and Eleonore obviously didn't agree with that. Since their second meeting, she noticed that sometimes Richard had some kinds of emotional outbursts.

The gardener turned his leaf blower off under unambiguous moaning and walked away.

"You can be quite loud." Eleonore faked a smile to hide how shocked she was.

Richard stared into space. After one or two seconds he looked back to Eleonore.

"Sorry, but it's important that I can understand you properly."

"Thank you, darling. You are so considerate."

Eleonore could not have faked her lady-like response better. She would have liked to praise herself.

"Eventually, Sophie entered the room. It must have been her because of her figure and her amazing hair. She wore a platin-blonde wig. I didn't check what time it was, but I was certain it was Sophie as I recognised her immediately. I just saw her blue dress glittering because of all the lights in the club. She was just so beautiful. It looked like she was flying over the dance floor with her high heels. She looked like a vision, just like a ghost. Many people turned over to look at her, and you could see women looking at her, envying her. The two men, who were apparently bored by me and our conversation, got up and their dangling jawbones reminded of two diggers on a construction site. A horrific scene I had only seen in cartoons before. They talked to each other in Arabic, and I don't understand this language. However, I know perverted men when I see them, and I can only imagine what they talked about while they repositioned their crown jewels again. 'Ehw!' is what I call this behaviour."

Eleonore picked up a pastry and tapped a few of the crumbs off of her blanket.

She paused for a bit. Apparently, she wanted to emphasise the main bit of her story.

Richard felt slightly dizzy and lifted his hand up to his forehead.

"Are you okay, Richard?", asked Eleonore.

"It's the wind. I feel a bit more delicate as I normally do."

Eleonore didn't spend much time worrying about what he just said. She poured a bit more tea into her cup and continued her story.

"I only saw them for a second before I left to go home. Sophie and the two men left through the entrance door. She didn't even say hi to me, nor did she thank me."

Eleonore waved her hands through the air as if she just did a magic trick. There was a bit of appal on her face because of how Sophie treated her.

"They left? Last time you said they went outside."

"Yes. They left. I didn't want to tell the story more fantastic as it already is. I went to the bouncer, who was almost two meters high and equally as wide and asked him if Sophie mentioned something to him when she left. He replied: 'Which Sophie?'"

Slightly irritated, she nodded with her head.

"I then went to the head of the bar and asked if he maybe saw the two men I came to the club with."

She shook her head again.

"He said he didn't pay attention to it."

Eleonore remembered the situation, and she saw in her head how Sophie laughed, and the two men romanced her. Sophie looked like she was distanced but beautiful at the same time. She wore a blue sequin dress paired with a blonde wig with long hair, which she put up in one wave. She was certain: This woman had to be Sophie.

Her French wasn't the best, but she understood, even despite all the noise in the club, how both men talked to Sophie about how impressive this club and her looks were.

Eleonore looked at Richard, slightly desperate.

"Do you know this situation when only you know what happened and only you can tell others about it, but no one believes you? Do you know what I'm talking about?"

Something was changing about Eleonore's face while she spoke. Richard thought he had to write it down. It looked like there were two different Eleonores and both shared one body. One of them was the crazy Eleonore who lost touch to reality, and the other one seemed to be the deceitful and maybe even frightening woman who was far more intelligent than the first version.

Richard didn't reply to her question, but he was seemingly touched by this outburst of emotion. For one second he was back to the beach with the family with the two girls. One of the girls cried, and her mother comforted her. The girl wore a plastic unicorn in her hair. This memory was stopped by Eleonore clicking her fingers.

"I decided they walked out on me, so I ordered another Gin Fizz before I headed home. I parked my car at the Sendlinger Tor. I can't remember where exactly but somewhere around the hospital. As I had a couple of drinks, I decided it would be best to take a taxi."

This explanation seemed a bit weak as she only mentioned a couple of drinks.

"Only a couple?"

"Nah, I bet I had four of five drinks."

When she saw the look on Richard's face, she added.

"I am not a drunkard."

"I didn't say anything."

"Fuck you. I saw the look on your face."

And there she was again. The angry Eleonore came back to the surface.

"Wow calm down. If there was a certain look on my face, I didn't do it on purpose." Richard wasn't surprised by this outburst as many clients go through ups and downs during his sessions. He acted like always and just ignored it, but he was, as you say, suspicious.

"It's okay." She found her lady-like role again, but there was something about what just happened that didn't seem to fit to what Richard was expecting.

"I took a taxi home that night and, although it was late already, I decided to take a shower, and after that, I went to sleep. I wanted to go back to the agency at about 2 pm. I texted Jenny if she could substitute for me at the reception. This was only natural as I needed to take care of the evening event as well, so I really didn't have a reason to go back to the agency so early."

"That's when you had a dream."

Eleonore nodded.

"It was only a dream, however, mixed with what happened after that, I think the dream just amplified my condition."

"Tell me again what happened."

"It was nothing special, but I rarely dream, ever. And if I do, I never remember it afterwards. But this time I dreamt of Sophie who went for a walk with those two men along the Isar, the river that runs through Munich. She floated along the river, just as elegant as she was in the club. Both men were entranced by her beauty and didn't dare to touch her with their hands. It was a mixture of admiration and fear. Her beautiful, big, green eyes looked into theirs, and she invited both to have some fun with her at the river.

She was so alluring in my dream, I even thought about becoming a lesbian for her." It was too late for Eleonore to realise that she just talked about deeply personal feelings.

Richard waved his hand to signalise that she should continue talking, and she did what he wanted her to.

"As both men came closer to her, they kneeled down, and Sophie lifted up her dress as if they …" Eleonore pointed both her index fingers towards her vagina.

"You know what I mean. Show this. Brr. As if I'd ever show my most intimate spot to those cave dwellers. Not even in my worst nightmare."

Eleonore pulled a face of pure appal.

"But you know it was just a dream, right?"

"Yes. I woke up at this part, and I am sure I watched TV for at least one hour until my heart stopped beating that fast."

She got a bit more comfortable on her chair and put the bitten croissant back onto the plate.

"Those croissants are very dry today. But well, when I went to work, I asked about those Moroccans and Sophie.

Nobody knew anything about it, and apparently, Sophie wasn't invited to the gala. That was the point where I didn't care about those Moroccans anymore, and I stopped worrying about them. Or instead I should have looked after my own work. It was weird that everyone started laughing when I said I saw Sophie."

"Where have they been?"

"Exactly. That is the question I asked myself as well, and as I thought they should come to the presentation in the evening I called the hotel. The people from the hotel only told me that they haven't seen anyone from Morocco.

"So?"

"Maybe they checked out the day before; however the receptionist said that she only seldomly sees hotel guests as everything is electronic today and they only have to check-in and out online. Well, now I asked myself when exactly they should've checked out because, as I said, I went to the 'Inferno' with them. You remember, don't you?"

"Sure."

"The receptionist told me that, if it was who she thought it was, they handed in their keys at the check-out box last night. She also signalised clearly that she couldn't tell me their names."

"What exactly is a check-out box?" Apparently, Richard didn't visit hotels very often, so Eleonore explained it to him.

"It's a box where you can throw in your room key to check out. It's super convenient when you're in a rush. In hotels like these, however, you don't have keys but code cards."

"Weird." Eleonore didn't know if Richard was talking about the situation or the code card. She didn't think he knew much about modern facilities.

"Right? I asked if she was there when those two men left the hotel and she replied that maybe there was a colleague who worked during noon. However, the room of the men she was talking about was empty for two days now. She then asked me if I wanted to make a reservation. I thought we reserved the room already.

I ignored it and only told Anne, who typically controls everything. I started my preparations for the following night.

I couldn't stop thinking that those two men needed to be driven to the airport and that they should say goodbye before.

I then went to my computer, and as I know that men like them are into posting everything they do, I searched for their profiles which I bookmarked in my browser before."

"I don't ever post anything. I don't think there's anything online about me, is there?"

Eleonore ignored what he just said and continued.

"Their profiles were gone. However, looking for them, I found something suspicious. Six years ago, both of them were in trouble because they attacked a tourist in Morocco. This was published in a French magazine.

There were four entries about this topic, but they were in French and another four or five in Arabic. I suppose the search engine translated my search keywords.

Richard nodded like he knew what she was talking about. Honestly, he didn't even know that a browser was able to translate information.

Richard suddenly felt a heatwave from his head to his feet, and he felt dizzy again. He looked down to his watch and contemplated if he should take a taxi instead of taking his own car.

"I looked for pictures and details about what happened, and I found an article where they published a picture of a man who was described as a tourist from Germany. This man pretended to be a woman and the two Moroccan men dragged him home six years ago."

Eleonore realised how a slight sign of discomfort became visible on Richard's face. She added:

"Transsexuals." With both hands, she pointed towards her crotch. Richard took a deep breath and nodded. This is how Eleonore realised that Richard really was homosexual. Holding back like this was typical for those men.

"Something seemed to have gone wrong with their appointment. When they saw that this woman wasn't really a woman, they took a knife and mutilated their genitals.

On another picture of this article was the victim with the perpetrator next to it. If I'm correct, the men were acquitted of the charges as the transsexual tricked them into believing they were a woman. They had to go to prison for ninety days. Apparently, it was against some religious regulation or something.

The story became tragic when the tourist died of an infection while waiting for his trial. With all the dirt in the prisons of countries like there this isn't surprising, isn't it?"

Richard didn't show any sign of emotions. He just nodded to show that he's listening to what she says.

"Anne looked at what I found online and explained that I misspelt their names and that we shouldn't show those articles and suspicions around. We shouldn't harm our agency with unproven rumours. I gave up and acted like I approved of what she said."

Both knew that Eleonore would've never stopped looking around. She squinted her right eye and pointed with her right index finger towards it. An Italian way of showing that she understood there was more to the story than what eyes could see.

"I did my own research at home on my own computer and, although there wasn't much to find in Germany, there was plenty to read in French from France and Morocco. The man who was mutilated by the two men got stabbed in his genitals several times after he was sexually abused by them. During the trial, the judge and the defender agreed on a suspended sentence. The victim either died or fled. Articles disagreed on the latter."

For the first time, Richard was obviously interested in her story. After she mentioned the stabbing of the victim's genitals, he checked his own discreetly. Eleonore thought it must have been a typical male reaction to such a story.

"What did you find out?"

"I can only suppose, but I knew that I couldn't find anything else at the agency. Anne tried to avoid the topic, and no one else knew about it. But let me tell you about what happened at the agency. You will agree that something is off – either with the agency or myself."

"What do you mean?"

"I was sure those men came to get revenge. They were monsters, and if my research was right, they were those perpetrators from Morocco. I think I saw them again later. I can't guarantee anything of what I say is right at the moment."

"Where?"

"I didn't say anything about what I found out at the agency. I wasn't sure if those two men really were who I suspected them to be. But they looked like them and phonetically, their names matched as well. I randomly read something about an incident on the motorways in Paris a few months later in an online newspaper. In this article was a hint that two Moroccan guys, who toured the country on their holiday, had an accident. I saw the picture, and it was hard for me to tell if it were the same men, but their names were similar. I have to admit, I can't always recognise this southern type, but I was sure it was them. The article was published on a Moroccan blog in France and seemed trustworthy. The car they drove on the motorway A 75 had problems with its stirring wheel. They drove faster than 180 hours per kilometre and lost control over the car on the bridge of Millau. For me, this was the end of the story about those Moroccan guys, for now."

Richard didn't show any emotion which confused Eleonore slightly.

"So? Those men were monsters. They got their revenge and in the end, justice won. I hope I wasn't involved in the revenge of them guys. I wish I could understand them. That's when I had an idea, and I looked through the pictures of our agency at the time of the incident in Morocco. And that's where I found something."

"Aha!"

"Definitely aha. I found a picture of our CEO Mr Brenner, and he looked similar like the victim in Morocco. I realised, Mr Brenner and the Honourable Sophie looked quite similar to each other as well. They must be siblings."

"Ah. This is how it happened?" Apparently, Richard wasn't entirely convinced by her story and tried to convince Eleonore of the reality, or at least he tried to bring her closer to it by asking her questions.

"I wanted to approach Sophie and asked around in the agency where I could find her. Everyone laughed at me. They told me Sophie was only invented by some picture-editing software."

"Yes. Mr Brenner told me."

"I'm not crazy. There was a Sophie. I'm sure. I didn't drink that much, and I can remember everything else as well.

"Leo, listen to me first and calm down. I can only work with facts, and we both have to deal with the facts I have."

Eleonore nodded.

"The Honourable Sophie is a product made in software. Anne showed me how she created her, and Mr Brenner only used his face because he's the owner of the agency. He most definitely is not a transvestite. You already saw him. He's good looking, but I couldn't imagine him being a woman, could you?

I hope you don't make me ask him to show me his penis, right?" Eleonore could see some of Richard's tiredness on his face, and she tried to ignore it.

Eleonore smiled and nodded. Richard continued.

"I suppose because of your loss of reality, you mixed up some information, which led you to believe that you saw this woman."

"No", whined Eleonore. She was close to a crying fit. She looked almost defaced and gave the impression of being close to an emotional outburst

"Calm down, my dear."

Richard waited until she recovered.

"Could it really be that I just imagined the whole story?"

"You're the only person who saw those men. The hotel didn't have any record of them being there as well."

"Anne…", protested Eleonore. She wanted to say that there was a folder named Al Jadida Duo on Anne's desktop.

"Anne is a very nice girl. She showed me her computer, and I couldn't imagine that someone who draws manga and collects unicorns would have the guts to make so many documents disappear. You show evidence of being stressed. You're fantasising about some conspiracy although it was proven not to exist. That's a sign of paranoia."

Eleonore seemed to accept this explanation only reluctantly.

"But how could this be? The folder was gone!" Richard couldn't reconstruct this hint as they never talked about Anne's desktop before.

"We can't approve those experiences, but we have to follow those thought patterns. I couldn't find the online articles you were talking about as well. I looked through your computer when you ordered me.

The site www.sweet-unicorns.de doesn't exist either or, at least, doesn't respond. I even looked the address up on my computer, just how you wanted me to.

By the way, you can have the keys to your home back."

Richard got the keys out of his pocket and handed them over to Eleonore.

"I remember that when I was a little girl, I experienced something similar."

"Are you sure?"

"Yes. I will talk about it later. When I was eight years old, I experienced something, and no one believed me either."

"What was it?"

"Not now." She held up her hand, and Richard understood that she needed some time.

"Do you want to take a break?"

"No. Today is the day I finally want to end this imagination. Now, listen to the accidents of a hunter in the Bavarian forest."

Angela looked down at her feet and saw that her left foot was bleeding slightly on the outside. She used Gazou to clean her foot and smiled for a second.

"Thanks, Gazou."

The river was further away then she expected it to be. She already walked for more than three hours, and still, there was no river in sight.

It got dark quickly, and she was tired already. She needed some sleep. Angela was also slightly hungry, and she contemplated what to eat.

Finally, she heard a stream and went in the direction where the noise came from. When she arrived, she drank the water which tasted moody. She washer her injured feet in the cold water and sat down for a bit on the small meadow. It had to be an allotment garden area. She knew that she was on the run and couldn't be seen.

Angelika backed off a bit and looked at the small wooden houses. She realised that none of them lived any people.

She tried the first house, but its door was locked. She went to the next one, and when she arrived at the fourth one, she could only barely see her feet in the dark. But finally, she was lucky and found a key at the garden light next to the door. Maybe it was something she did as well in the past. She didn't know. But it didn't matter, she opened the door and looked for the light switch.

"No, Gazou, no. If someone saw the light, they could catch us again."

She groped in the dark and found a sofa. It was a bit wet and felt just as uncomfortable as the bed she had where she was before.

She was too tired and fell asleep immediately, even without any blanket.

Angela dreamt about a day at the beach and how much she was looking forward to being with her family. Everyone was talking and a girl, she forgot her name, gave her Gazou.

"Thank you, my dear. What's his name?"

"Gazou. The magic bear."

She wasn't sure if Gazou really was a bear as the puppet wasn't made very well. However, she made the girl happy and so she gave Gazou a welcoming kiss.

She couldn't see any faces in her dream. It looked like everyone was grey, without any faces or names.

Angelika continued her deep sleep, and she couldn't remember anymore. She woke up with the first ray of sunlight.

"Gazou", she whined, "my feet are hurting." Gazou just stared into space with his small button eyes and didn't show any emotions.

"Come on. We want to go swimming. Come on. Wake up." She shook Gazou fiercely and got up.

Soldiers

Bavaria is a traditional state in southern Germany. Its people are filled with pride and are very welcoming. There are many small forests around its capital Munich. Despite the growing population, you can see wilderness in those forests. Although many say that Germans don't have as many children as expected, the number of people living there increased steadily. Issues like housing shortage are one of the most popular topics in the city's newspapers. No one ever reported the same about the poor animals living in the forests.

In many placed in Bavaria, there are still hunting associations, although game and small animals are almost exterminated. Bears and wolfs are extinct, just like lynx and the real beaver. Nevertheless, those associations claim their profession and sport as necessity, like nature couldn't regulate itself.

The association "Holy Hubertus" had been in Wolfratshausen, near Munich, for more than one hundred and thirty years. Apparently, back then, a confidant of Kind Ludwig II belonged to its members. Every Thursday, the hunters met in the inn "Gasthaus zur Girglsquelle". During those meetings, they talked about in inaccessibleness of their lives, got to know each other, as far as that was possible, read their agenda and spoke about the planned activities of the association. Throughout the years they didn't only learn how to shoot and kill animals, but they now also knew about renaturation and the return of land to the animals, and about other social activities like baking Christmas cookies or painting Easter eggs. It's worth mentioning that they never actually gave land back to animals. The only reason why it was worth discussing was because of advertisements in brochures where they could ask for donations.

Otto Meiersdorf was the chairman of this association of hunters. During his normal life, he worked as an ordinary auditor without much importance or necessity in his company. However, in this association he was precisely what he always wanted to be: an important man. As the successor of his dead father, he ran those meetings every second Thursday in the month. He assigned tasks to his following who end the lives of vulnerable animals every six weeks. At his feet under the table sat his dog Wauzi, a restive dachshund who fitted perfectly in the picture of Otto's role at the association. Wauzi seemed to have more sanity and trust in the other members of this association than Otto himself, but this wasn't debatable. On one evening, Otto sat at the head of the table and read the weekly newspaper out loud while Wauzi huddled up against his feet.

"Blimely!", swore Otto. "There's another weirdo from the animal welfare who behaves ragged."

The mixture of Otto's Bavarian dialect and the use of standard German indicated that he wasn't happy with a complaint from somebody who complained about the actions of his association.

Otto was always glad to explain that he was fluent in "Bairisch" which described the language and "Bayerisch" which meant the political attitude, but not the language. People who moved to Bavaria within the last years didn't seem to know this and Otto always took the opportunity to start emotional speeches and remarks.

"Listen! This weirdo wants us to cancel the fox hunting because of the accident with the dog."

For the third time already, an innocent came to grief. It was a dog which walked around in the woods and got shot by one of the hunters who thought it was a fox. The association wrote a few letters of apologies and the owner of the dead dog received a new puppy as compensation. However, there were still raging protests against the hunters every time they planned a new event.

Otto just laughed about this letter and handed the writing on the pink paper around. Summarised it said that a woman, probably one of the protesters, wanted hunters to look after nature and urged them to realise that animals, no matter how old or young, also had a right to live. She also stated that foxes, just like dogs, are friendly and trusting animals and that they aren't a threat to society.

Sayings of their members pointed out dead boards and ducks. They painted outlines on the menu.

With a beautiful handwriting, the woman continued to call on the consideration of the declining numbers of animals in the forests of the region. Despite how friendly the letter sounds, she picked her words wisely and ended the letter with a fixed ultimatum.

"Someone ordered her from elsewhere", noted Otto as he addressed his first secretary and recorder or the meeting.

Every year, this woman wrote to Otto, and it was the same every year. The Green parties received more and more members who, according to Otto, all had unrealistic perceptions. Otto was member of the conservative Christian party and, although he never did anything for the associations he was part of, except his own hunting club, those memberships should undermine his character.

Even references to the Christian Franz von Assisi who had mercy on animals didn't convince Otto.

"If you can't consider my request in the program of your association, I ask you for understanding the following measures in advance", Otto mimicked the standard German of the woman. His round chin danced along his fat throat while the pulled an ugly face. He was convinced the woman was as old as calligraphy and the choice of words was too formal for the younger generation. He then showed everyone how he would wipe his bottom with this letter and handed it over to his secretary.

The waitress had to interrupt their laughs and knocking on the tables as she wanted to serve boar with potato dumplings. The loud circle then ordered wheat and pale beer and a lemonade mix, and the waitress noted everything efficiently.

"Hey, I will reply to this woman super friendly but with a big 'Kiss my arse' in the end." Peter-Anton Weißhaupt was the youngest hunter and, although not many people knew about it, he wasn't an animal lover whatsoever. He traded fur with countries from the North, and it happened several times already that the press picked up on this in a very negative way. Fur rivals protested several times in front of his store close to the Viktualienmarkt previously.

His woman died four years ago, and since then he lived with his son Meinrad. No one really understood Peter-Anton. It happened only rarely that he laughed, and he was very reliable in his job, but he always looked at the floor when he talked to somebody. Everyone thought he was hiding something. Secretly, he only wanted to kill and used this sport to hide it. This affinity was concealed by the argument of it being tradition. Not many people understood what was really happening.

Hatred and bitterness, created by a forced wedding and a life full under the pressure of his father and father in law, turned a once happy boy into a seething volcano of emotions which could erupt any second. His dialect from Lower Bavaria was hard to understand, but when it came to the critics of this association, he could handle them in formal German. Everyone agreed, and the young hunters already picked appointments for their next meetings. At those meetings, everyone wore Lederhosen and a felt hat and the girls were pretty in their Dirndl, the Bavarian dress. Since the upcoming change in generations everything became some kind of show rather than traditions.

Peter-Anton lived in his own world, where he didn't expect resistance or punishment. This is down to his excellent relationship with the police and local politicians. However, once, he made a horrible mistake. He underestimated the power of revenge and the loving words of a letter.

The evening went by as expected, and only Peter-Anton had a special task which was writing the protocol. His son always accompanied him to those meetings. He was already fourteen, and he would be taught how to shoot soon. The boy was named after his grandfather. He was cheeky and very self-confident.

They replied to the woman very superficially and the week went by without anything suspicious until the day of the excursion.

One day before the hunting, nature lovers came to the site of the association and protested against weapons and the killing of animals. Gutto Linde lead this protest. Their posters were bright and grammatically completely off, but they wanted to do something good for animals.

Gotto's actual name was August, just like his grandfather and he already knew about his godson's nickname. He formerly was the leader of the protest group. His partner Arnaud took pictures of everything and wrote notes for a newspaper article. Arnaud was a well-known photographer and a freelancer at the local newspaper. He was always lucky and got to every accident in the region on time to take pictures there.

Just like the woman warned in her letter, the protest did happen. Otto and his colleagues didn't expect it to such an extent. Other than posters and pamphlets, they also brought animals and pictures of Basco, the dead golden retriever. They remembered everyone about the incident when Peter-Anton gave in and got caught. The police officer, a friend of Peter-Anton, trivialised it to be so-called material damage as, legally, a dog is treated as a thing. This caused even more protests against the police who therefore backed off from this case.

On the evening of the protests, some dogs seemed to be trained to howl passionately and for a very long time. It was so annoying, the hunter's association had to cancel their meeting. Everyone ordered just one more beer and went to the toilet, but the protesters seemed to be relentless, and the dogs must have thought everyone wanted to hear another round of howling.

After twenty minutes of further howling, Wauzi und Bella decided to join in the dog choir from under the table. This led to Otto losing his temper.

He quickly announced that they could kill six foxes and parted the group in two smaller squads. They planned on meeting at the grove in Wolfratshausen near Munich at 6 a.m. The annoyed hunters quickly paid the waitress and hurried to their parked cars while avoiding the protesters.

Arnaud took picture after picture. He captured how the environmental perpetrators sneaked out of the inn and how one of the protesters aimed with his own vegetables to hit a girl who just left the restaurant. Protests about their individual rights were ignored, and every member of the hunting association managed to sneak out of the inn.

The restaurant was empty just thirty minutes later, and only two half-drunken guests ordered another Schnapps.

At the next day just before dawn, some of the hunters parked their car next to the usual meeting point and waited for instructions of Otto, their leader. Usually, Otto wasn't late but the protests on the prior evening caused additional work, and he had to call several other politicians to make sure that there won't be any more trouble.

They checked every safety measure and their weapons.

They walked towards the forest in two groups, and Peter-Anton neglected their leader's instructions by bringing his son Meinrad.

Although Meinrad was only allowed to watch, he still pushed through his will despite his worried fellow hunters.

Meinrad just thought it was too early. Moisture and the cold forced its way through his coat, and he would've rather stayed home where he could shoot deer in his computer game.

They walked through the woods in the south of Munich. They brought six dachshunds, one of them being Wauzi, and a female dalmatian which accompanied the hunters on this wet but gloomy day. Because of all the excitement from yesterday, the dogs seemed very stubborn and not very interested in hunting foxes today. The hunters tried to encourage them with pieces of fur on which the dogs were supposed to sniff on. Bella, the female dalmatian, pulled on her leash and howled very loudly. It was the first time ever in her life that she did that. Gerlinde, Bella's owner, laughed and said proudly that her dog must have taken on a trail.

However, Bella and the six dachshunds decided they didn't want to go any further and started howling together. It sounded just like the dogs of the protesters the day before. Wauzi didn't seem to be able to howl so he made a yodel noise which amused many of the hunters.

Otto decided to leave the dogs behind as all the foxes would escape because of the loud noise they made. The hunters brought their dogs back next to the cars, now very annoyed. Gerlinde and Otto's wife Sabine were supposed to stay at the cars to watch the dogs and Meinrad. The remaining hunters left and tried to forget what just happened with their dogs.

"We'll talk about the bowling evening where we defeated every man." Sabine proudly announced that she, as the leader of female bowling, had some plans for the following week. Last Thursday, she won bowling despite the twelve Schnapps she had. Now she was bound to be elected to be part of the board of this group.

The wet and gloomy clouds of fog were lower and denser around the trees today, something that didn't happen very often at this time of the year in Bavaria. Usually the fog disappears when the sun rises, however, on some autumn days it might be that the sun rises later or sometimes not at all. The hunters didn't want to cancel today, and so they went further into the woods. One of the younger ones moaned that he would catch a cold soon and everyone giggled quietly in response.

Otto led one of the groups and pointed with his finger where they had to position. Peter-Anton led the other group and didn't care too much about Otto's instructions. Clearly, it was a war of power between those two men. No one said it out loud, but everyone knew about it. Otto, who was scared he got competition for his position in the group, gave instructions which were ignored skilfully. If someone asked for Peter-Anton, the response would be something like this:

They both knew each other since being children as their families lived next to each other, but today, they didn't have many nice feelings towards each other anymore.

◆

Peter-Anton was in a slightly worse mood today, and Otto's constant instructions got to him a bit too much today. When he noticed that he was further away from the group for a minute, he enjoyed the silence. He pushed some snuff tobacco up his nostrils and sniffed its smell. For a moment he forgot about the dispute in the association and looked around nature. The fog seemed to clear, and he followed the trail deeper in the woods. He was sure he would soon reach the Loisach, a river leading in the Isar, or, even better, a beer garden in this forest.

A few memories came up in his mind in which he tortured animals until they were dead right in these woods. When he was younger, he let out all his anger at those vulnerable animals. Anger because of his dominant father, because of his forced marriage, because he became an unimportant man. No matter for what reason, several animals had to suffer because of it.

He shot Basco, the golden retriever, deliberately. The dog tried to stop him from finishing torturing a fox. The fox and Basco didn't survive the day.

He was sure he couldn't ever get turned in with the police, and the small material damage with the dog will be paid by his association. "Material damage" it is called if a vulnerable dog is killed brutally as if his life was less worthy than human being. Thoughts like this tantalized the last moments of poor Franzi's life.

The path seemed to just wait for his steps, and even the cut-down stocks looked like they were positioned on certain places like on stage. The light falling through the trees, the open glade and even some wet leaves seemed to be placed on specific positions. Everything looked like on a picture of a holiday catalogue.

A dull noise next to him reminded of the sound of slowly deflating balloon. A stock rolled from left towards the right and forced him to jump to the side. A dark cloud covered his surroundings, and his eyes stung. A bit of this pain was probably because of his hay fever, but now they stung even more as if he rubbed his eyes with his dirty dingers.

"You did come to hunt." A magical voice caught Peter-Anton's attention. He turned around and looked for this voice.

"I'm here." There was a brown-haired woman together with two big dogs standing surrounded by the trees. The dogs could be Afghans. They were too pretty to be hunting dogs and too well-groomed to be going on walks through the forest. Peter-Anton couldn't assess this woman. She looked young, but still, she was of a certain age. Her body didn't look typically female, she was skinny and tall. Too tall for a woman actually. Her coat was moss green, it looked heavy, and it hung down to the ground. He was so surprised; he didn't know what to do. His nose was itchy, and his eyes were tearing up. What a bad combination. A hay fever attack and a female stroller in the woods.

Ornaments covered her body and stressed her athletic figure. She was a mixture of an Artemis and a goddess of revenge who was hidden behind shiny eyes.

"What are you doing here?", he asked, surprised. "Who are you?" he asked without waiting for her to respond to his first question. He tried to sound commanding as she shouldn't be walking around in a forest where they hunted anyways.

With one movement, the brown-haired woman opened the button of her coat on her throat, and it fell down to the ground. Her body was exposed, and it showed many scars. In the beginning they were only visible on her throat and her hands, but they were all over her body. Instead of falling to the ground, Peter-Anton thought it looked like the coat vanished between all the leaves. She was naked underneath, and her skin looked like covered in pearl and leaves. He was convinced that her genitals were distorted. Peter-Anton wasn't sure what it was, but definitely not an ordinary woman.

Peter-Anton's heart started to beat faster and harder than usual, but it was more down to his arousal than to be scared. The woman strutted around wantonly while the camera took pictures of every second of her show.

She must be crazy, walking around like this in the cold, Peter-Anton thought.

'Why is this perverted transsexual here in this cold forest?', he thought and wanted to look for his group, but his neck decided not to move.

His eyes wandered off to her perfectly shapes breasts which were framed with some leaves and traced the glamorous movement of her long and beautiful legs. Her dogs moved to both sides of her like they would be dancing synchronously around her. He thought about whistling to get the others attention because otherwise, no one would ever believe him.

"You're crazy!", he heard himself saying but his voice failed. The brown-haired woman came closer and kissed him on his lips. She smelled like moss, wet mushrooms and animal urine but still, she smelled alluringly good. He was frozen and felt dizzy and numb.

Until now, he never got a kiss from a man, let alone a transsexual. He was frozen and horrified at the same time. He wanted to protest and push this disgusting person away, but his body seemed to be numb. The moment of surprise mixed with some kind of inexplicable arousal. In his imagination he would like to do the same to this transsexual what he did to a badger some time ago. Thinking of hurting her gave him Goosebumps.

"Are you aroused, my dear?", the woman said in a slight baritone.

His gun fell to the ground, and his heart was beating heavily, but this time because he was scared. His hand moved in the air, and he vainly tried to grab his gun, but after grasping into nothing twice, he gave up. For a second he thought that this weirdo might have put drugs on his lips or that they got something planned. Maybe she was one of those nymphomania, transvestite girls he read about in the newspaper or heard of on his meetings with his fellow hunters. His eyes flickered, and the fog seemed to clear. His body was filled with a mixture of curiosity and fear.

He heard how the photographer walked around him and the transsexual. He jumped around like a satyr as if the ground was his stage and he was the new Vaslav Nijinsky.

Peter-Anton thought that this female transsexual was much more interesting than everything else he saw before.

Click, flash and another click followed the movement around him, but he couldn't turn his head, so he didn't see the photographer anymore; however he knew he stood behind him.

"I warned you", whispered the beautiful lips of the woman.

Peter-Anton could move backwards slowly, and so he distanced himself from this woman. From a distance he could hear Otto screaming around his usual rants and giving instructions to the group. He wanted to run, but at the same time, he wanted to admire this woman. He noticed every detail about her body and how she looked in the forest.

He fell and lost his felt hat. He crawled back on all fours and wanted to go home again. Obviously, this transsexual had to be crazy. She was naked in the cold, and she looked like she rolled around on the ground in the woods before. The feeling of fear which so many animals had to live through because of him now seemingly reached him. His knees bend, and he felt his sphincter jerking. Yes, he thought, she had to be a homeless, horny thing. His thoughts were too perverted to be said out loud. He quickly jumped and wanted to get hold of the transsexual, but his legs didn't do what he wanted anymore. He felt a dog's canines plunged into his calves like a dagger.

He felt how he got tortured slowly, just like he tortured a badger in the woods more than ten years ago. He remembered how he abused it and how he broke its legs with his boots. He felt the dogs pulling him back and how they breathed at his throat. They tortured him and didn't leave any traces.

The moisture of the woods got through his shirt, and the smell of old moss made him fight for air. He continued crawling, and just before he lost his conscience totally, he managed to scream.

Meinrad lingered around the edge of the forest. He was extremely bored and looked around. Wauzi only got out of the car after numerous loud protests. Gerlinde couldn't stand his yodelling any longer. Wauzi looked for tracks in the bushes and every now, and then he scratched something with his paws. Meinrad was a good friend, and he threw him some sticks, but the dog didn't care too much today. Again, Wauzi started making loud noises, but this time, he ran into the woods. Gerlinde shouted for Sabine, Otto's wife, who just had to quit, and she hurried after Wauzi into the woods. Meinrad joined, just for fun. Wauzi caused some distraction, and everyone was glad they had a reason to move in this cold weather. Bella was confused. She whined and shivered slightly. As she was more submissive than Wauzi, they let untied her leash and took her with them. But this time she wasn't as submissive as usually, and she quickly ran in the same direction as Wauzi.

The wetness ran down the leaves and caused some movement in the trees. Like every morning, the birds were singing and banished some ravens. Ravens were dangerous opponents, and it was harder to keep them away for smaller birds, so they all sang together while the dogs vanished in the woods. Gerlinde and Sabine found some strength, although they were tired from bowling last night, and followed the dogs into the forest.

Sabine saw Wauzi in the far distance how he was more agile as usual. He jumped from one side of the path to the other and revolved around himself like he would try to catch his tail. Uncertain if he should jump or hunt his tail, Wauzi ran into the woods on the left. As the women arrived there, they saw Bella, who waited a bit but now continued her running. They were slightly out of breath and realised they needed more exercise. Lise, who until now remained in the car for them, was faster and sprinted behind the two women and caught up with them.

Wauzi jumped several times on his forepaws as if he would give them a sign about one hundred and fifty meters into the woods. His copper-red fur was full of dry leaves, and he looked like he was desperate for a bath.

"Are you crazy, dog?" Gerlinde pointed her finger on his snout. Lise, however, didn't care about Gerlinde instructing the dog. She ran towards Peter-Anton who lay on the ground, sweating and shivering.

"Gerlinde, Sabine, help me. He lost his conscience." Sabine was busy with her handbag and at this moment, she was slightly embarrassed.

The Bavarian women were small but definite and grasped Peter-Anton under his arms. They were strong and confident and managed to carry him with a lot of puffing and whooping, back to the car. Meinrad approached the group. As he saw his father who got carried around, he was shocked, lifted up Wauzi and followed the group back to the parking space. Sabine forgot about needing the toilet and her handbag and helped the others carrying Peter-Anton. Behind him, Meinrad noticed a shadow in the forest. At this moment however he didn't think of anything else except helping his father and if possible, not crying. A true Bavarian man shouldn't cry in this situation, he thought.

The women let Peter-Anton fall to the ground next to the car. Lise already looked like she collapsed. Her pretty embroidered scarf hung down to the floor, and her Dirndl came undone on one side. Her hair was a mess as Peter-Anton's arms were lifted up in his unconsciousness and he ruined her hairstyle. She couldn't deny her overweight as she was fighting for air. Gerlinde, who already raised two children, was more used to situations like these and she looked for injuries on Peter-Anton.

"Can you drive, Lisa? I can look after him, but I can't drive a car", she apologised and spotted a small injury on Peter-Anton's leg. "Oh dear, he got bitten by a crossed viper."

"Oh lord, why exactly is a viper going to come out in this freezing weather?", asked Lise annoyed. She finally managed to get some air back.

"Look at it", Gerlinde showed her the injury to defend herself.

"Such nonsense. Let it be, push him up to the car. Boy, you stay here, and you tell the others that we brought him to the hospital in Stockdorf", commanded Lise who, from experience, immediately stroke the right tone. Gerlinde already bushed this tall man into the car and Meinrad forgot about his fear and was okay with holding the position. The other dogs got out of the vehicle already because of all this confusion. Led by Wauzi, they sat around and watched with indecisive joy what happened.

Meinrad watched how they drove away with his father and stayed with Sabine. Like all good Catholics, they prayed that God will look after him. Even if there actually was a God, he didn't listen to Meinrad at this moment.

◆

"Leo." Richard listened to her story and tried to imagine how much of it was actually true. After a short break, he continued.

"In your condition, it's common to have such imaginations. Now, that you have told me such an extraordinary story, you have to tell me, no, you have to explain to yourself why anyone would try to get justice like this."

"I told you that I'm fighting for animal's rights. Others are just like me, who think animals are vulnerable and exposed to our moods."

Richard was used to having such conversations without much hope and logic, but something in the way how convinced Eleonore was made him feel uncomfortable.

"I really can't prove that everything happened exactly like this. However, I'm telling you everything I remember, or whatever is in my head. That's what you wanted me to do, I didn't", Eleonore defended herself.

"Sure. You're right. I just didn't think your stories were so fantastic."

"Everything has its own logic."

"So, do you know how much a campaign like this would cost? Looking at economics isn't irrelevant either, right?"

"If you consider what you charge per hour." Eleonore nodded and laughed. Maybe Richard would've joined in, but he understood it more as criticism and took it too personally. He didn't show it, but Eleonore realised she did something wrong and continued telling her story."

"I suppose that maybe different wishes and dreams came together in my life, and I transform them into this fantasy."

For the first time, Richard was happy about what Eleonore just said. It seemed like she was slowly starting to think about what was real and what belonged to her fantasy.

"Is this now where your … let's say … imaginations end?"

"Oh, no." Eleonore waved her hands in the hand and put off this thesis.

"No way. It continued, and I'd say it even got worse. But I read a lot in the newspapers so maybe this engaged my fantasies."

◆

Peter-Anton was hospitalised right after his accident in the woods in the local hospital in Stockdorf. The doctor came to the conclusion that he hit his head while falling and now he suffered from hallucinations. It took three months until they finished the final lab result. It stated that Peter-Anton came in contact with devil's berries, scientifically called Atropa Belladonna. This plant was known for growing in this region and most of the time, touching it was avoided. According to the doctor, Peter-Anton probably stroked the plant with his calve, and through the injury he experienced poisoning. The doctor's colleagues grinned after hearing this diagnosis, but no one dared to voice another theory, as they didn't have one. They also thought about it happening because of the Psilocybe semilanceata, known as liberty cap. As mushrooms are only in season between September and October, this theory didn't make sense, and so the other doctors decided not to disagree.

However, the amount of scopolamine in his blood was very high, which lead to him experiencing delirium and then led to a coma. All doctors nodded knowingly, but they all knew that this wasn't enough explanation for the condition Peter-Anton was in. The concentration of scopolamine was too high to be natural, but even in the chemistry lab, they couldn't determine or explain where it came from. Peter-Anton was transferred to a care home. A few weeks later he woke up from his delirium but except his urge to draw what happened to him, they couldn't find out anything else. Within only a few weeks, he couldn't move properly, and his body vanished like a mirage. Eventually all that was left of him was just a shadow of a formerly smart man.

Peter-Anton was a skilled artist. In the few moments, he was awake during his stay in the care home, he took coal and paper and drew the same shape of a woman, accompanied by two over-dimensional dogs. There were eighty-seven pictures in total, each picturing other details. Sometimes he drew her with luscious lips resting over a round chin or with two almost ideal breasts covered with leaves, or he drew the two neat dogs standing next to her. Meinrad was sure that dogs like those didn't look like the dogs his father would've liked. Bavarian men like dachshunds, dalmatians or nowadays Jack Russel terriers. Their dogs needed to be fierce and submissive. Those toffs which needed hairdressing didn't have a place with former Bavarians.

Peter-Anton didn't say much while staying in the care home. He expressed himself with his pictures and was depressed because of a few memories of dead animals. Meinrad falsely misinterpreted them as hunting trophies.

Meinrad realised that his father was obsessed. He didn't know much about his father back then, but he did know that he was very sexually active. In Bavaria, this is a topic no one would ever talk about at a family do or between father and son. The country is extremely Catholic, and all body parts between the belly button and knees weren't stated in any dictionaries. This was a repercussion of Pope Pius IX's fig-leaf law. He single-handedly hammered out every penis of every statue in the Vatican and replaced it with a fig leaf made of plaster. Some still ask what a priest does with a box full of stone penises, but this isn't a topic in Bavaria either. Meinrad just knew that after his mother died, his father bought a big collection of porn videos and not only seldomly, he heard unchaste moments though his father's bedroom door.

After what happened in the woods back then, Meinrad lived with his uncle in the house of his parents. His uncle looked almost exactly like his father, but he was ten years older and about twenty kilograms heavier than him.

His uncle took charge, and he was very attentive. His name was Augustin, and he took Meinrad to church every Sunday. He probably never said a prayer, and he certainly didn't know the paternoster, but he did what he could to provide everything for his brother and looked after his nephew.

Peter-Anton lived for another twelve months in his care come until he gave in. As nobody wanted to spend money on investigations and his insurance didn't provide any money either, doctors restrained a diagnosis. The untold secret that no one really knew what happened to Peter-Anton died together with him.

Together with his uncle, Meinrad picked up his father's legacy and prepared the discharge documents. Discharge included the actual handover of the dead body to the undertaker, but it was called discharge, so the document doesn't sound like a death certificate.

He stood in front of eighty-seven pictures and thought about where and how he was supposed to store them. The drawings were detailed and painted with a lot of devotion. He knew those pictures couldn't belong to his father's porn collection. 'The hottest in the alp hut' and 'Horny in the Geyerwally' were probably of other proportions.

Meinrad sold and swapped a few pornos with friends from school, but everything had to happen very secretively. His uncle didn't want to look at the collection. He wasn't as open about his sexual activities as his father.

"It's sad to see what is left after he died, but I am sure it was best for him. I think your father didn't even realise he died", said his uncle Augustin who stood in the door. There was great sadness in his voice.

"Those paintings are gorgeous and apparently the last things he remembered. I will put them all in a folder, and we'll leave them in the attic together with his other belongings. I will get someone to dispose his clothing locally." During the last few years, Meinrad lost all the love and connection to his father, but still, his death shocked him.

The fellow hunters of the association disappeared in the woods after what happened. Apparently, the dispute between Otto and his father cast a shadow on him.

Otto was Meinrad's godfather, but this fact was celebrated formally once or twice a year, and otherwise no one mentioned it. He came around for Christmas and his birthday but other than that Otto didn't show up for Meinrad.

Everything went exactly as traditional as always. The urn with Peter-Anton's remains was buried in the family grave.

The funeral was small and only a few neighbours and relatives Meinrad barely knew showed up. Otherwise, no one came.

This is how Peter-Anton's story came to an end, and the hope for a sweet ending was lost. After the funeral, Meinrad went home and bought the daily newspaper at a kiosk to cut out the death notice.

"And how do you know all of this?", asked Richard. He obviously didn't feel well after listening to her story.

"Mr Brenner bought those pictures after Peter-Anton died. Arnaud must have heard of this case, and I am not sure how they became friends; however he apparently asked Mr Brenner to buy those pictures. Mr Brenner owns a gallery. I was part of the protest against hunting and hunters." Eleonore almost sounded like she would apologise.

"What do you mean by buying?"

"After the death of his father, his brother noticed that the woman on those pictures was the woman of out advertisement campaign from three years ago. It was about the perfume Acqua Vergine by Celestine. You know it, right?"

Richard rarely applies perfume, and he didn't use this one for more than nine years now.

"It was a long time ago. I think the last time I used this perfume in the male fragrance was a few years ago. "

"I am sure your legs weren't injured by then?" Richard blushed. Apparently, he didn't understand the joke, or his humour was too sensitive when talking about his legs.

"How did you get this injury?" Eleonore was aware of her mistake and wanted to make up for it with this question.

"It was during an insignificant accident but were here to talk about you. We shouldn't change the topic."

"Sure."

"Arnaud it the photographer of 'The Valley' right?"

"Yes. Gutto is his partner for the light and the stage scene. Arnaud is German and grew up somewhere at the French border. I did my research on both online."

Richard knew that Eleonore apparently spent a lot of time researching online. Now he was interested in hearing which connections she found.

"Tell me what you learned."

"Well. It is like Mr Brenner said. Just pure coincidence but after almost every protest organised by Gutto, there is an accident with that very environmental criminal or fur trader. I compared eight different results on our Social Media pages with the animal protests organised by Gutto. At five of those an accident or something worse happened. Especially after the death of Peter-Anton."

"There are vast connections on which you base your allegations, don't you think? You think Arnaud harms those people?"

"After all those five incidents Arnaud went to the hospital. A motorcycle accident, falling with his paraglider or after a ski accident. Suspicious, right?"

While Eleonore spoke, she remembered pictures of those accidents where Gutto planned his protests as well all the visible scars on Arnaud's body. In her perception, they crossed a line where they went too far with their animal activism so that it wasn't safe anymore.

"How do you know of Arnaud's scars?"

"The pictures of his wedding trips show his definitely well-trained body and how he hugs his skinny Gutto. Both men are captured in swimming shorts, and his scars are very visible."

"Well, well. That means you think small Gutto is a dangerous animal activist as well?"

"Somehow I think so, yes." Eleonore placed her index finger at her chin and Richard could see that she genuinely considered this possibility.

"But Gotto is a small man. I knew him, he is funny and cheerful. I'd never think he's a dangerous monster."

While Richard was speaking Eleonore had to picture a possessed Gutto who forces the head of an owner of a fur farm in the mud until he drowns. A few days later the newspaper only talked about one victim of the floods at the Lusatian Neisse – a poor farmer who wanted to save the lives of his animals. All the animals escape into the forest, but the farmer didn't make it.

Eleonore seemed to contemplate if a picture like this might only be a result of her imagination and she decided not to voice what she was thinking about.

She remembered another incident in North Rhine Westphalia where a farmer issued the killing of ten thousand geese because the payment of the insurance for a fake poultry plague was better than letting the goose live for another year. Gutto walked down the entrance hall in a rage and frantically called other activists. Twelve days after the protest the farmer who killed the geese died in a tractor accident. Imagining this made Eleonore shiver. Using the tractor as an avenger angle, Gutto would have driven over the screaming farmer.

"Leo!" Richard called for Eleonore's attention. She didn't seem to realise the long pause because of her small brainstorm.

"Sorry. I was caught in my own thoughts." She waved her hands around her head and pulled a face to indicate how crazy she must seem.

"These are nice and happy men, and you have a morbid imagination in my opinion. We found good explanations for everything until now, didn't we?"

Eleonore pulled up her scarf a bit more.

"It always slides down. Please, be nice and get me to brooch off my make-up table. The one looking like a dragonfly covered in amber." Eleonore pointed her index finger towards a dresser next to the bathroom door.

Richard heaved himself unwieldy and went to the dresser. Once he got there, he stared at the implied ornament.

"Yes, I know. It's not the prettiest piece I own, but it was cheap. I bought it at a flea market at the Olympic tower. Do you like it?"

For a moment, Richard stopped smiling, and his fingers touched the dragonfly made out of fake amber.

"Where did you say you bought it?"

"I won't give it to you. On a flea market at the Olympic tower, you know which one, right? It was on the weekend."

"Yes, oh well. I just thought about a friend. It's her birthday soon."

"Ah, I see. Well, in this case, I'll give it to you." She looked at him from the side and closed her eyes partly as if she discovered a secret.

"Oh no, oh no. Not this type of friend."

Eleonore took the ornament and thanked him silently while she tried to secure her scarf with it.

"To convince you, I might have to tell you about the story of our costume designer."

"I don't know it yet", confirmed Richard.

"It will open your eyes. Sandra, a woman from Brazil, came to Germany, thinking she would become a famous dancer. She dreamt about a career in the national ballet, but it didn't go as planned."

Angelika was tired, and she knew it was a long way until she would reach the river.

She rested on a clearing for a moment. A woman who walked her dog looked at her with horror. This woman misunderstood the situation apparently and thought Angelika was homeless.

Her bottom and the hospital dress became wet because of the grass. She sat Gazou right in front of her.

"This woman is stupid. Who wears white shoes for a walk in the woods?"

It was obvious that these weren't Angelika's best years but the woman with the dog didn't care and hurried along the path in the forest without looking back.

Angelika could recall her last day in her hospital slightly.

"Mrs. Wiemer", she was greeted by a man in a dark suit. He must have been a lawyer or one of the better-off visitors.

"What's the point of all this?", asked Angelika.

"Court ordered us to have a conversation with you."

"A conversation? What about?"

"Please, don't feel offended. It's a conversation we'd rather have in your office."

Angelika couldn't recall the details of these conversations, but she remembered that those men weren't accountants nor lawyers.

"They told me I wasn't allowed to keep the hospital", Angelika explained to Gazou.

As Gazou didn't reply she moved his head, so he nodded approvingly.

"Exactly. They said I am crazy and that they held everything in trust for me."

Angelika started crying for a moment and she realized nothing belonged to her anymore.

"In trust."

She cried a bit louder and teared her hair. She shook her head a few times and cried more heavily. A married couple who went for a walk in the woods looked at her, pulled a face and walked faster to escape the sight.

She remembered that everything happened because of her good-looking husband. He certified her insane and assumed everything himself. They had a marriage contract which clearly stated that he wouldn't succeed her but as long as she wasn't dead, he was her guardian and he could do whatever he wanted.

As the fog cleared in her head, she realized that she would sit in this cellar until she died so her husband could manage her assets.

"Betrayal." She said it like she overcame her hebephrenia for one moment.

'What happened to my girl?' Angelika knew she had two daughters. It could've been two girlfriends as well. She wasn't sure anymore.

Angelika got up and took Gazou. She walked towards the sun as she knew the river had to be there.

She sang and danced along the path and everyone who crossed her way avoided her. No one seemed to realize that she was a woman who needed their help.

◆

Dummies

Sandra, a woman from Brazil, Rio de Janeiro, looked at the suitcase on her bed. She wondered how fast she could walk while she carried the weight of this case. As a memory of Rio de Janeiro, she left a sticker of the local check-in on the suitcase. She never went on a plane before flying to Zurich and everything was really exciting for her. Now she looked down at a situation which she never wanted to experience. She especially hoped no one from her family will ever find out about it.

"I will need about an hour to carry this suitcase to the train station." She talked to herself. She needed to train her talking skills as she was alone. She looked at the broken wheels of her suitcase and thought that she couldn't afford a new one. It wouldn't be easy to carry the suitcase either. She knew that.

She wore short jeans. They were so short; parts of her butt were visible. Beneath them she wore mash stockings which chafed her crotch. She didn't care about her uncomfortable outfit in this moment.

She tied up her formerly thick hair in a bun as she couldn't afford to go to a hairdresser.

She opened her suitcase again and looked at everything, contemplating if she really needed all of this. She picked out a small backpack which she folded up to make it fit. She stuffed the toiletries which were packaged in a washbag of a discounter, in the backpack, together with a pair of trousers and a jumper. She couldn't stand the cold as she never experienced any temperatures under seventeen degrees in her home country. In Frankfurt it had about eight degrees at the moment. She contemplated how long she could survive in her shorts outside in the cold. She packed away her other belongings again and pushed the closed suitcase under her bed. She had to secure the case with a lock as it happened quite often that a colleague just took something for an unknown amount of time.

Four weeks ago, she asked for help in an online forum for women where she contacted someone called AliciaKee. AliciaKee seemed to be known in many women's groups but no one actually knew her in person. Sandra's only freedom was that she could browse the internet in Portuguese in an internet case. Otherwise, she always had her watchdog looking over her shoulder. She didn't even browse the internet on her phone as her boss or the guards checked it regularly.

She contacted a group which apparently dealt with hopeless cases like hers. Her case was truly hopeless. She didn't have any of her papers, no money and she was monitored all the time. She was on the margins of her existence and she was scared to go to sleep every night. When she was told that a lawyer will contact her, she thought about fleeing.

Her lawyer was called Paloma and she told Sandra that a trained person will pick her up to get her out of this hotel. Today was the day they agreed on. Sandra was meant to be picked up today to go to a fashion show.

Sandra smiled at the idea of turning up at a fashion show, styled like this and only barely dressed.

They instructed her to delete messages on her phone immediately and to follow the instructions precisely. The group who focused on rescuing hopeless people was an alternative group, which had a very strict idea of affiliation and administrations. Sandra didn't understand everything, but she knew that she had to leave this place very soon.

She looked around in her bedroom and she teared up slightly, but she didn't want to start crying. She didn't want to ruin her make up with her tears and so she pulled herself together and took a deep breath. She was supposed to go to one more show. She thought about how she wouldn't ever participate in such a show. Except for the opening of a shop in Rio de Janeiro where her friend presented cheap beach fashion. She didn't have the spark she always wished for in her current life.

She felt slightly sick because of the smell of artificial room scents which accumulated in the walls of the hotel. The walls of her room were painted in an eggshell yellow and full of spots. They were as monotonous as her former day to day life.

She couldn't believe her luck when she was approached by two blonde guys at the beach of Ipanema two years ago. They invited her to go on a trip to Europe. They asked her after one of her shows for tourists on the beach during the Sambadrome. Many dancers dream of the moment when some manager discovers their talent. At least on this day it seemed like it was her time to be discovered. However, the bitter truth was that they were just looking for fresh girls for their business on the German market for forced prostitution.

They told her that they came from Frankfurt, where they owned an after-hour bar with many guests of the surrounding banks. Only manager and high-ranking employees of insurance companies and other financial giants came to this bar. Sandra couldn't tell the difference between a German or a Russian accent. That's why she incorrectly assumed that both men were German businessmen. She didn't even think about the integrity of them as she knew there were good and bad people in every nation. The illusion of those two Russians, or whatever they were, was only the start of what waited for Sandra in Frankfurt on the Main.

In the beginning, Sandra thought it was funny that there were two cities called Frankfurt in Germany. She bought postcards with pictures of Frankfurt on the Oder instead of Frankfurt on the Main as she kept confusing the two cities.

So, she also assumed that a bar including shows in Frankfurt would be the same as in Rio de Janeiro where it is about entertainment and not cheap sex. She hoped, or dreamt more likely, of a clean environment with well-payed shows. Her imagination grew and turned into phantasies where she would wear pretty costumes and expensive jewellery.

All those dreams were destroyed on the first day when she arrived in her room and the men took her passport from her. She finally understood that this entertainment bar is nothing than a cheap brothel where women didn't wear much and had to pay for the shreds, they wore themselves.

She discovered that those men were Russian and that they knew how to turn the mindset of reluctant girls. Some of those reluctant girls suddenly went, let's say, home for an unknown period of time or on a long-time holiday where they couldn't ever write a postcard from. One of those girls was found dead at the shore of the Main, covered in bruises. Her dead body was so battered, they could barely say who it was. The policeman who interrogated the employees of the bar enjoyed seeing the shocked faces of the dancers. He didn't think about the girls just being more scared and actually giving more power to the two Russians then before.

Her phone vibrated.

'Take only the necessities. Fifteen minutes left.'

She deleted the text as agreed and ordered. She opened the backpack again, emptied it halfway and pushed everything under her bed again. She locked the case and turned the code back to zero, hoping that one day she will get it all back.

The home telephone in her room rung unexpectedly.

"Sandra", she answered it. The long A of the first syllable indicated she was Brazilian. Many people really liked her accent but right now, it slightly trembled of fear.

"We need you at the bar. There are too many customers."

"Lischka, not now. I have … "

"What do you have? In case you're ill, you have to use condoms", interrupted Lischka with a harsh undertone.

Sandra thought this was very degrading and if her mother found out what happened to her having expensive dance lessons, she would probably cry herself to death. She wasn't allowed to call her home in Brazil and her mother wasn't there anymore to hear what Sandra had to say.

"No, Lischka. I'm not ill, I have to have a shower because …"

"Because what? You're not drunk, are you? Do you need help?

A threat. Help was a synonym for threat. Her phone vibrated.

"I will be there in thirty minutes. I just have to get ready."

"I will send Miroslav to your room in twenty minutes."

Lischka is the oldest prostitute in the bar and she managed to have a relationship with one of the Russians. Although she was a victim of forced prostitution herself, she kind of found a way of surviving where she didn't have to suffer as much. But the downside was that she made other women suffer even more.

Sandra looked at her phone.

'Track 23, section B in 10 minutes. Leave the hotel.'

Sandra looked through the window onto the street and spotted a small man who could only barely be seen under his purple hat. At the entrance to the back yard, next to the big bin, she saw a woman who unbuttoned her coat.

The message was short, and she had to hurry through the lobby onto the street without being seen. The back exits of the hotel were behind the kitchen onto the back yard where the bins were. Employees weren't allowed in the kitchen. She decided to leave her coat and to walk out of the door in her short outfit. She'd rather risk catching a cold then getting caught.

Meanwhile, the computer at the counter didn't work. There were more than twenty orders for escort girls. Normally, they didn't even have twenty orders per week so Lischka was slightly nervous.

It could also be that the Armenians thought it was funny to send all those girls to a non-existent address.

Lischka called both her assistants and tried to get an overview about which of those orders were real.

Sandra deleted the text, took her bag containing money and her phone and went outside on to the hallway to call for the elevator.

Right after she clicked the button for the elevator, she noticed her high heels. She realized that running in those would be too dangerous. She hurried back into her room and threw the shoes under her bed next to her suitcase. She was desperate and took only two cheap flip-flops which she brought from Brazil.

The elevator was as slow as always and the doors opened with a metallic sound of the old gears. Sandra hoped that it wouldn't stop working today as she knew it would be time for it to break down soon. During the last months she got stuck in it three times but walking down the stairs from the sixth floor and breaking her neck wasn't an alternative. The stairs were old and narrow. Accidents happened frequently.

'Cameras', the thought as the wind caught the elevator and made it shake. The thought of someone watching her came into her mind. She hoped Hassam, the janitor, fell asleep in front of the TV again or that he was busy playing cards on his computer. It almost made her fall over when the elevator arrived with a loud bump on the ground floor. The door wouldn't open properly so she had to help it manually.

Sandra could hear Lischka screaming Ukrainian orders to her gorillas in the back room. Every now and then she laughed so Sandra thought something good most have happened.

Currently, only twelve girls were working at the bar. She saw four of them approaching the door and assumed they got an urgent order.

"Hassam", she called her colleague at the reception.

The old man sat at his computer and played cards. He only briefly looked at her to act like he was interested what she had to say.

"The elevator is broken again. I'll go to the drug store. I need deodorant."

"What deodorant? I told Ishmir to put new one in your room. Did you not find?"

Ishmir was the chambermaid. She wasn't suitable for any other services because of her look so she had to clean the rooms.

"Hassam let it be. I don't want to smell like cheap Shalimar."

"Shalimar is good perfume. My wife uses it for many years and I still really like the smell."

"You're too old, Hassam. I'll be back in ten minutes."

Hassam was dealt with, she thought triumphantly.

She talked to herself quietly while walking and didn't look at Hassam again. The glass door opened automatically, and she saw one of the Russians at the door. It was Miroslav.

The taxi driver talked hectically, and a fifth girl had to come outside and went into the car. Sandra quickly looked at the driver and realized his strong body under his very tight shirt.

A few girls were busy so it must have been her and further six girls in the bar as one other girl was at a customer.

The man with the purple hat on the other side of the street called someone on his phone and laughed loudly while talking. The woman who Sandra saw through her window earlier didn't seem to be around here anymore.

"Where are you going? Lischka wants you to be on stage."

"I just called her. Miro, I will be back in a second. I just need two things from the drug store."

Miroslav's face didn't seem to move at all.

"Miro" cried Sandra. "It'll only be five minutes."

"You're almost naked and in plastic sandals", Miroslav said after he looked at her from top to bottom.

"So? Am I supposed to wear an evening dress?"

Sandra realized that she didn't look suitable to go out on the street, but she had to make to best of her chance to run away. After preparing this day for three weeks now, nothing could go wrong.

"What? You look like a slut."

"You're right, but that's why I will be back in a second and I will dress up just for you."

She knew how to beguile men and Miroslav wasn't too smart, so he believed her.

She walked towards Moselstraße in the direction of the underground and just wanted to cross the street when Miroslav shouted her name.

"Sandra!"

She shuddered and heat spread in her body, her knees shivered, and she panicked. She prepared to run away as Miroslav's strong hand packed her back on her shoulder.

Sandra looked into the bar and realized that there were only three girls. Apparently, everyone had a busy day and they all went to their customers.

"Are you deaf?"

She jumped and tried to stay in role.

"I'm back in a second. Don't pressure me so much, man. Ohuw! You're hurting me."

"Here." He handed her a note.

"What is that for?"

"Buy a pack of cigarettes for me, would you?"

"Oh, cigarettes." She laughed again but slightly hysterically as she realized her mistake.

The man with the purple hat crossed the street and walked away from the hotel.

Her phone vibrated again. Sandra got scared and tried to silence it to act like everything is like it normally is in front of Miroslav. In all this chaos, she lost control over her phone and it fell to the ground.

"Did you snort cocaine or what's your problem? You're so wired today." Miro bended over to pick up her phone for her.

"I'm in a hurry, give it to me. I have to be back soon or Lischka will be mad at me."

Miroslav picked up the phone and read the text which was visible on her lock screen.

'I see you. It is cold.'

Miroslav wasn't the smartest, but he could sense that something was off here.

"Do you have a lover?"

Sandra panicked massively and thought about an explanation.

"Miro, it's just a friend. She wants to lend some money off of me and I'll be back in a second." Her acting lessons had to pay off, she thought, but her show didn't convince Miroslav.

He held her arm and forced her back into the direction of the hotel.

"Miro. You really don't have to do this, right? I just wanted to meet her quickly and I'd be back in a second. I'm not dressed properly either."

"Shut up."

Sandra heard how something was moving on the left side of the entrance.

Miroslav pushed her back into the hotel. To the right was an entrance door to the dance bar where the girls were supposed to encourage bored men.

Normally, all the girls were booked online or via dating portals but from 5 p.m. onwards clients came to the bar who didn't want to go online.

They walked past the door to the bar and right into the direction of the office.

"Miro!", screamed Sandra but he didn't seem to care.

Miro asked for Wielki, who was number two of the organisations, by nodding his head towards him. Wielki was in the office, left to the bar entrance.

Lischka, who looked after everything, jumped off of her chair at the counter and walked towards Miro.

Now only two girls were at the bar as the third one was ordered by a man to come to the door. They had a cigarette and talked. Sandra was nervous and she wanted to be freed by Miroslav.

Stories of slavery in Brazil went through her head and now she could imagine how brutal it must have been back then.

"What's up?", asked Lischka.

"I think he has a lover and was about to meet him." He handed her phone out to Wielki.

As Wielki wanted to unlock her phone he realized he couldn't.

"Turn it on!" He gave the phone back to Sandra and ordered her to unlock it.

There were small drops of sweat on Sandra's dark skin because of how scared she was. There was sweat on her upper lip and she could smell the scent of her body. The strong scent of sweat indicated how scared she was.

She could hear the background music of the bar in the office as well. It wasn't the best music and the blues sounded like a Greek singer who now started an endless howling. Together with the red light in the room it gave the impression of being in hell.

Sandra's fingers didn't listen to her anymore. They trembled and she vainly tried to unlock her phone. Before she could try for the third time, they stopped her.

"One last time and you will get the night off."

This meant that they would beat her so much, she wouldn't be able to offer any services to her customers. She had to survive this procedure six times before already. It was weird that, after they beat her up and she couldn't work, she still had to pay for her room.

Sandra took a deep breath, tried to concentrate and unlocked her phone.

"Here you go." She handed it over to Wielki.

She slid over her touchscreen and couldn't find any texts.

"Did you delete the text?" Wielki asked Miro but Sandra thought he was talking to her.

Meanwhile they received more and more orders and Lischka sensed already that something was off.

"This weirdo pushed me all the way over here and I don't even know what he is talking about. How am I supposed to delete a text if I don't even have my phone, smart arse?"

She couldn't have known that she loses her nerves and so she talked to Wielki patronizingly. For this behaviour she was rewarded with a thwack on her cheek. She fell on her knees and noticed a small injury in her mouth, but they didn't seem to care.

"Don't do this here. Go in the kitchen!", ordered Lischka and pushed everybody out of the office where you could look in from the bar.

Miroslav picked her up from the ground and they carried her into the kitchen without her touching the floor once. She lost her flip flops on the way and they just left them on the ground.

"Don't scream. You already know what could happen, right?"

Sandra couldn't live another day in this horrible bar and she'd rather die than getting another blue eye.

Her phone vibrated again.

'I'm coming to you.'

Miroslav and Wielki talked to each other in Russian or something similar. Sandra couldn't tell the difference between those languages. She just knew that sometimes they spoke Russian, and other times Ukrainian. No matter how, they weren't happy with her and she knew that they found out what she wanted to do.

"Who's that and what does he mean by coming to 'you'?"

Wielki showed the text to Sandra and she nodded her head.

"I don't know what this is about. I just wanted to meet a friend."

, Подготовить себя к мучительной смерти', the phone vibrated again.

Wielki read the text and instinctively hit Sandra's face again.

"Who is sending you those texts?"

Sandra looked at it and didn't understand anything of what happened here.

"I don't know what this is. It's not Portuguese."

"Sure, silly cow, it's Russian. It says: 'Be prepared to die in pain'"

Everything calmed down over the last months but the conflicts with Iraqi pimps and drug dealers could become a habit again. That's why they were careful not to let their girls get in any contact with them.

Both men switched back to Russian and this time, Sandra was sure it was Russian. The last hit heated up her cheek and she tried to control the dizzy feeling. She felt like she would faint any moment. There as an iron taste in her mouth and she knew that meant her mouth was bleeding.

Miroslav got an automatic gun out of the halter he hid under his left arm. They started talking in Russian again and Wielki called for the only assistant in the kitchen. They opened the door of the back entrance.

"Who did you want to meet? Talk to us or you won't survive another hour."

The phone vibrated again and Wielki read the new text message.

‚Ty tozhe net!'

"What does he mean 'We will neither'? Who is this?" For the first time there was fear in Wielki's voice. There weren't any ruthless murders in this business and most of the time everything is calm. However, he knew that Miroslav and himself weren't prepared for anything worse.

Wielki was tall and his short-cut hair looked like from a soldier. It clearly showed that he could assert himself with his body, but he wasn't very trained. Under other circumstances Sandra would've even described him as a handsome man. But in this moment, she just wanted one thing, and that was to survive.

She saw a petite woman in the backyard of the hotel. She looked like she would walk her dog. The dog was small with short hair which was almost completely white.

"You and your mutt", said Wielki harshly "Leave!"

The woman wore a dark red hat and her long, dark blond hair looked almost red in this bad lighting. She wore skin-tight clothes which made her look like she would be on her way to the gym, Sandra thought. She bended over to whisper something unintelligible to her dog and unleashed him. Wielki wanted to keep talking but once the woman undressed her top, he was speechless.

"You have to talk to Lischka", said Wielki who clearly was confused by what happened.

The woman was almost too skinny, but she pulled two strings on the sides of her trousers. She pulled them up until they were above the button of the trousers. They zipped through the air and the fabric fell to the floor.

She stood there, completely naked and, even despite the bad lighting, she was clearly visible. She was covered in tattoos in different sizes and colours. The two strings looked like heavy steel cables which she quickly swung around her. One of them wrapped itself around Wielki's throat and as he pointed his gun on her, she wrapped the second cable around his hand which pulled him to the floor. Sandra was nervous but she knew it couldn't be steel. She wanted to start screaming, but she didn't know who could hear or help her.

The gun fell to the ground and Wielki rolled over on his side. Sandra was too surprised by what happened, she leaned against the wall and looked shocked with her eyes wide opened. She didn't know whether she should be scared or relieved. She indecisively tried to judge the situation while the back door of the hotel opened again, and Miroslav and the chubby kitchen assistant came outside.

One of the cables the tattooed woman swung around caught Wielki while he tried to get to his feet again and it made him fall over again.

Sandra screamed but then squeezed her hands in front of her mouth and tried not to be in the way of the fight. She realized the woman must have been helping her out of this situation.

The small dog jumped on top of the bin which stood next to the door. From there, he jumped on Miroslav's throat. He barely had time to notice the attack by the dog which now jumped back to the floor and went back to the side of the tattooed woman.

The woman swung the two strings around like two steel whips and managed to hit the revolver out of Miroslav's hand. The assistant jumped towards her, but he didn't reach anything except one of the whips. The woman jumped directly towards him and bit his neck like the death fairy. With a front flip she jumped onto Miroslav's shoulders. Meanwhile, the small dog, which actually proved to be very strong, looked after the assistant who lied on the floor, bleeding.

Sandra wanted to scream again as the woman placed one leg on Miroslav's head and broke his neck with in just one move. The blunt noise of a breaking bone made it clear that Miroslav wouldn't ever be able to get up again.

Wielki recovered from the attack and kicked the dog. But instead of whining because of the pain, the dog carried on attacking him. Wielki barely saw what happened after that because the woman stepped on his head so harshly, he banged it against a wall for one last time in his life. He didn't die, but the step was aimed for him to be petrified for the rest of his life.

The assistant seemed to try to run away, but the unknown woman wrapped one of the strings around his throat and pulled it tight until he became unconscious.

All three men were laying on the floor and Sandra hoped not to be the next victim of this furious woman.

The woman let go of the chef, went towards the bin and opened a backpack which laid on the ground. She got a cloth out of the backpack.

"Hi Sandra. I'm Jenny and this is Chopin."

"You're naked."

Jenny cleaned herself with the cloth and put on her blouse again.

"That's true and it's cold. But we don't have any time to talk about clothes."

In the meantime, Jenny created a wrap dress out of the two parts of her former trousers. She wrapped the steel whips around her hip and Chopin was leashed again.

"Are they dead?"

Jenny looked around and the bleeding assistant seemed to be unconscious now. She picked him up and threw him back onto the ground.

"I bet he is. The others are free to tell everyone about my performance."

Jenny looked around again and corrected herself.

"Well. This one can tell about it. The other one was too soft."

Jenny walked towards the assistant and pulled her skirt tight on its sides.

She picked up the chubby man with one hand by his collar. The tendons in her arm tightened and looked like they were about to bust. Her other hand pulled his hair. He whined and tried to scream but his growing fear seemed to freeze his scream in his throat.

"Do you understand me?"

He nodded quickly.

"You now walk into this direction and you'll never come back. If I see you again ..." Jenny nodded her skinny chin towards dead Miroslav.

The assistant was barely able to get up, but he moved as fast as possible. On his way to the gate, he had to crawl on the floor several times.

"We'll probably never see him again", noted Jenny. She was completely dressed now. Chopin seemed hurt on his side. Jenny massaged his legs and he thanked her with a dog kiss.

When Sandra looked for help online, she didn't expect a fighting woman. She watched Jenny wiping some drops of blood off of Chopin and fought for air.

"Oh God. What are we doing?" Sandra couldn't have hoped for or imagined what just happened.

"A few women are able to do Capoeira in Brazil, but I can't do anything like this." She quickly left the backyard. Jenny put on her coat which she left at the entrance to the yard. Sandra's tension made her talk a lot.

"I learned Kung Fu and later Capoeira. But I soon couldn't do it anymore. I am too old for this."

Sandra looked at Jenny's body and tried to figure out how old she must be.

"Forty-one."

"Sorry?"

"That's how old I am."

"I am ashamed." Sandra's voice was unsteady while talking. Obviously, she was shocked.

"Don't try. You're not prepared for anything of this. But we have to leave."

They already reached the corner of Moselstraße and saw pedestrians walking back and forth in this shopping street.

"It doesn't happen very often that I have to take care of cases like these, but you were in horrible hands there."

"When I found your agency online, I already stated that I don't have any money and the Russians have all my papers."

"Someone else will look after your papers. We just have to leave now."

Sandra realized that the bar's door was shut, and she couldn't see any of the other girls.

She also saw the man with the purple hat checking the lock at the door and how he went inside of the bar. He took off his hat and she saw his cute, round face for a second.

"Why do you undress before a fight?" Jenny laughed when she heard this question.

"Blood on skin can be cleaned off better. If I burnt my clothes, I wouldn't have to undress, but men are always tricked by nudity. They don't know if they are supposed to look at me or to defend themselves. I'm sure those men here won't ever make the same mistake again."

Sandra could barely talk. She heard of other resolute Brazilian women who weren't scared of men, but she never thought they actually exist.

"But what if they hurt you?"

"Then I will get a new tattoo to cover it up. All of my tattoos cover scars from former incidents."

Sandra counted quickly. She found more than fifty tattoos or just a lot of very big scars.

"When I asked my lawyer for help, I expected a flight back to Brazil or living in a women's shelter."

"When you had those thoughts you didn't know that barely one woman survived this organisation in the last six years. They export women from here to somewhere else or they just vanish, and no one knows where to. You have to know that those women don't have any papers, no one misses them and when they're dead, no one would ever know."

Sandra realized that Jenny just described her situation in just one sentence. She might have been too old for this job soon or they would have found someone more suitable to replace her

As she understood her situation, Sandra almost screamed.

They reached the train station and Chopin happily greeted two other greyhounds which stood at one of the tracks together with a well-dressed woman.

The woman looked elegant and tall. As Sandra looked closer, she thought something was slightly weird, but she couldn't put her finger on it. However, this woman was dressed so well, her clothes were probably more expensive than the ones Sandra wore in her whole life. They were likely to be even more expensive than many of the cars Sandra ever drove.

"Please keep the dogs on their leashes", said a security guard from the train station in a loud and clear voice.

"Don't worry, we don't put our dogs in the dangerous situation of being too close to the tracks", laughed Jenny.

"Meet Sophie. Honourable Sophie."

◆

Angelika finally reached the river Loisach at its very top. She laughed happily and danced with Gazou as if he was her prince.

"Gazou", she said with a high-pitched voice.

"We made it to the river."

She wasn't in the best state and has been on the run from the sanatorium for two days now. In the first night at the garden she was still protected, however, last night she spent close to a stream. The wet and cold night had negative effects on her health. After so many days without her medication, she got a clearer picture of the situation she was in.

She didn't have the chance to protest when her husband decided to hospitalise her because of a mental disorder. Because of the medication she received after that, everyone who saw her thought she was crazy.

But it was because of the shock of betrayal why she ended up with hebephrenia and she couldn't deny it.

She didn't know much about her illness, but she knew that she didn't have a house to which she could come back to anymore.

During some brighter moments, Angelika realized that she was an old woman and it didn't make much sense to talk to a stuffed animal like Gazou.

She didn't have any money and she was hungry. A bad combination and because of the injuries she got while she was running away, she got weaker and her illness got worse.

She tried to remember who could help her now, but she didn't recall just one person from her earlier life. The only one she knew was Gazou.

Two crying girls were driven away from the house which nowadays is the sanatorium. Angelika remembered that one of them gave her Gazou and the other one was slightly older.

She tried hard to remember anything. She knew that her husband was good looking and a thief.

"Who were those girls?", she heard herself asking.

She put her feet in the cold water and relaxed. It felt like a remedy after all the walking she had to do.

"They weren't my daughters, as I can't remember having children. Can you, Gazou?"

Gazou didn't reply so Angelika shook her head.

"One was your friend."

She moved Gazou's head to he nodded.

"The thief stole all my money."

Again, Gazou moved his head like he nodded sadly.

"The thief was my husband." For a second she remembered him in her swimming pool.

"He didn't love me."

Gazou nodded again.

"He never loved me."

Suddenly, her memories came back.

"There was something in the juice", she said to herself.

"I gave her a sedative, but you should know that we should either keep her calm or we need to hospitalize her." The man who said this was a psychiatrist who her husband apparently ordered.

"I will take care of the administration of this institute, but you're right. We have to monitor her." She heard her husband talking but their faces were just grey and shapeless.

"Since we lost this girl, the only trace we have is this stuffed animal." The psychiatrist pointed towards Gazou. The stuffed animal laid on the table in her office.

"We can't say for sure that it has something to do with it."

"But you still know that since she brought this stuffed animal home with her, she behaved, let's call it, rather girly. A clear indication for the mental disorder which I diagnosed."

"You're right unfortunately. I'll bring her in the guest room and tell the nurse to look after her."

"The medication which I'll give to you should calm her down so the nurse's work will be easier as well."

"Thanks, doctor." Her husband put his arm around the doctor's shoulder as if they had been friends for a long time.

"As soon as I transferred the remaining papers into my name together with my lawyer, I'll send you the money."

"Don't worry, I trust that you will stick to your part of the agreement. It's to both out advantages, right?"

"Make sure to look after her because if you let her die, the institute will inherit everything and her remaining fortune."

"I trust I have the right employees. I'll just have to change the concept of this house slightly. We can't have as many people here anymore because of her condition."

"Yes. Sure."

The doctor left the room and a woman with a wheelchair came in. She knew this woman. She employed her but she didn't remember her name.

"Bring her to our guest rooms in the basement but lock the door when you leave. It's for her best, she could try to run away. We have to look after her now."

The woman approached her softly and was very careful when she lifted her almost dead body in the wheelchair.

"How could this happen?", asked the woman incredulously.

"We don't know if yet, but it looks like she had a shock. It could also be that the stress of the administration of this hospital was just too much. Who knows what it could have been? The main thing is that we can do the best in helping her now."

With those words she was pushed in the souterrain, which she wouldn't leave for a very long time.

She didn't know what kind of shock that should've been which she apparently suffered or who the lost girl was.

Angelika cried once she realized the reason why she wasn't dead yet.

But she had to focus to remember how she could have suffered of this shock.

Sandra got changed on the toilets in the train station. The Honourable Sophie handed her a bad with clothes and her coat.

She wanted to cry but Sophie's strong hands held onto her arms.

"No, my dear, you don't have any time to cry. Get changed and hand your old clothes to Jenny."

"You're transsexual", said Sandra without judging.

"And you're a whore." Both laughed loudly because of these mutual assessments.

When Sandra was dressed, she looked at herself in the mirror.

"How did you know the size of my clothes? Everything fits perfectly."

"I had a lot of dolls when I was younger. It was easy to guess your size."

Sandra relaxed for a second and almost collapsed because of the adrenalin rush.

"Here is your ticket for the train. You'll stay in a hotel for three days. Jenny will show it to you. Another employee will hand you out your papers and you can go back to Brazil."

Sandra was speechless and she realized that many people could only dream of a chance like this.

"Sophie, I can't pay you for this."

"Don't be silly. How could you pay us for this job?"

Sophie lifted her hands up towards the sky and her long fingers almost looked like claws.

"We all had to go through similar moments. No one of us is interested in money because we all have been so close to being dead, we could almost smell it."

Sandra knew that she wasn't far from it either as she was almost too old for this kind of work.

"Just one thing!"

Sandra nodded.

"Don't mention this night to anybody. You don't know us and if we need you, we will contact you."

Sophie paused for a bit.

"Sure. Sure."

Sandra took the train to the hotel. Jenny accompanied her.

Two days later she had her papers back and a ticket for a return flight to Rio de Janeiro. Once she was back, she was supposed to work as a model for the agency 'The Valley'.

Eleonore drove Sandra to the airport, and they talked about Sandra's experiences in Germany. Sandra cried more than she could actually speak. They were tears of joy and relieve at the same time. It led to an emotional outburst.

"Don't forget that you have work in Brazil, and we expect you to do your best for our agency."

Sandra avoided every conversation about Jenny and what she experienced together with the other women from 'The Valley'.

When Sandra was alone at the airport, waiting for her flight, she read the headline:

'Horrible accident downtown prompted questions'

On the front page was a big picture of the hotel where she was working in. Sandra had been living in Germany for quite some time now, but she didn't speak the language as well as she would've liked to. From the article she understood that there was a gas explosion in the kitchen on the evening she left the hotel. Two men got injured and one died on a broken neck because of the blast. A woman who just barely survived the explosion with just a broken arm and different fractures in her hands thanked police and emergency personnel.

The woman with the broken arm and hands was Lischka. She told the reporters that she fell in her office and parts of the ceiling fell onto her arm.

The police were clueless about the fractures in the hand of the bar chef. They apparently found traces of pliers. However, the woman denied everything and assured it was just a horrible accident.

On one of the pictures was a man in a purple hat. He helped a woman out of the debris of the bar into the ambulance. The pictures were labelled with the copyright of a photographer called Arnaud.

◆

"Those are quite serious allegations. If you're right, you'll have to talk to the police", warned Richard.

"The problem is that I can't say I actually experienced it. It could also be that I just dreamt everything of it. The only thing I know for a fact is that I brought those Brazilians to the airport, but it doesn't prove anything, does it?"

Richard was amazed by the fantasy and creativity; however, he knew that confronting her with the reality and the ghosts of her imagination would be a challenge he wasn't sure if he could take on.

"Leo. I can see that your imagination is very well-marked but your connection to reality might suffer because of it. Would you agree?"

"I'm not done yet."

"Sure, I know, and it has nothing to do with it but I know that we have to bring clarity to what is true and what is created by your fantasy."

"Well, I'd agree. There's just one story left which I have to tell before I'm done. Jenny and Gutto were part of it again and the story might help you to understand why I worry."

"Right, go on." Richard poured himself another cup of tea.

Clowns

It can get very windy in October in Germany. On one night during this month, Aca (pronounced Atchah) walked through the streets for a park at the foothills in Cologne. He was on his way to his apartment at the river Rheine. The wind came together with a few raindrops and it messed up his hair. He held his coat together close to his body. Originally, his family was from Fatih near Ankara in Turkey. Aca was born in Germany, six days after his mother came to the country.

Many teachers praised him during his time as a student and his German skills were a big help for his family. He could handle everything in German. From going shopping and answering the phone to dealing with all the billing-related issues of the family, Aca was able to do all of this since he was six years old. But all of those skills didn't help him in the situation he was in now. He held on to a charm with his left hand which was buried in his coat pocket. His sister Sögun gave it to him. She told Aca that his family got notice of his homosexuality by an unknown source. Aca knew that this anonymous source must have been a friend of his father who he knew from going to the Mosque almost every day. He met this man in a sauna in Cologne which was for men only. He apparently liked to be part of all the fun men had there, without stating too many details. When he realized Aca was there as well, he was so surprised, he quickly hid what was his contribution to the circle of men under his towel. He acted like he was at the wrong address and ran to the dressing room. Aca sharply looked at the bump under the towel which was quickly wrapped around his mature body. He indirectly told him with his looks that he understood a lot of what happened under it. Since this meeting he couldn't forget how cocky he was and that this will have horrible consequences for him. But this wouldn't have been much of a defence when he faced his father. Aca also knew that he couldn't ever go back to the Mosque as no one would help him there and his reputation, which wasn't too good anyways, would've probably run ahead of him. Since he was eleven years old, he knew, that he couldn't live up to his father's heterosexual expectations. When he was sixteen, he left his parent's home to live in Cologne where he found a new place in society as well. He cut himself off from his religion and tried to avoid the contact to his family. He only visited them during special occasions, as for example for Ramadan where his father insisted of him being there.

Aca wasn't surprised when his sister warned him that his family would clean the sin of his realignment in life with his own blood. For this reason, she asked him to stay away from all his relatives and friends from Mosque. Sögun and Aca were almost like twins. She also wanted to stay away from the traditions and start a carrier as a lawyer, however it was almost impossible for her. Her self-confidence cost her several slaps in her face by their domineering father. But still, she was waiting for the day when she could find the courage to break out of this circle.

When Sögun found out about the retaliation against Aca, she was devastated and talked to a few friends who also want to break free from the traditions of the Mosque and their families. She belonged to a new generation and she had new visions about a future where she didn't want to be a housewife or a mother of six children. She loved and respected her parents, but she had to stay away from their traditions. She explored all possibilities to protect her beloved brother. A friend recommended, she could write in a blog for women where she should state every detail about her family, Mosque and her brother. This blogpost should be forwarded to a Brazilian woman, that's all she knew about it. This woman was in Rio de Janeiro and lived in Frankfurt on the Main before that. The friend who got her in touch with this Brazilian woman, told her that this organisation worked in the background and it wasn't easy to find. She also warned that they might not be able to help her out of this situation. But it was worth a shot and so everything took its course online and Sögun prayed every day for the life of her brother and about the reconciliation of him and their family. She only received this charm as a reply which was ridiculous, but she didn't want to lose hope, so she forwarded this package to her brother, just like the cover letter of the parcel stated.

In the box where the doll was in, was a fairy-tale about the Brazilian Iara. Iara was a ghost of nature which lived close to the water. She pulled bad people into it and drowned them. It was the same story , just like in other mythologies. In Germany it was Loreley. The story was a bit different but Sögun didn't read up about it as she wasn't interested. Iara was either at the river or in the forest accompanied by two dogs. Sögun also thought about the similarities to Goddess Artemis. It seemed like every mythology in the world had the same story line.

Aca looked at the ridiculous doll made out of see-through glass beads which he got out of this pocket. He realized that the interior of the doll was harder and thicker than usual key chains or charms. But he did exactly what he was told to do, he carried it around with him, wherever he went.

He thought this was the last memory of his sister before something would happen to him. He knew he didn't have enough money to leave the county and the Mosque's networking was too tight to just run away. That's why the only thing he saw in the hope of his sister, was an inevitable goodbye of his family and maybe even his life. The police couldn't help him either and so he found himself in a situation where he at least had this doll with him as moral support.

Friends from Mosque contacted him one day later after he met his father's friend in the sauna. They told him they knew for a long time and immediately tried to find a woman for him.

Aca got the impression that having sex with a woman became some kind of remedy. Most of them just offered non-arrangeable sisters, cousins or friends for him to marry to save aliment and to put him under pressure. Aca also knew that if he ever married one of those women, he would be insulted and still, have to work for the livelihood of this house for the rest of his life.

The doll which he got from his sister was crafted rudimentarily and its legs were skinny and wiggled almost like it was dancing the whole time. For one moment he relaxed and smiled, imagining he would be dancing in Brazil, half naked with a feather boa around his neck, while men pushed a few dollar notes into his thong. He knew that no one in actually got dollar notes in their thongs in Brazil, but it was a funny picture and it almost made him forget the situation he was in. Three men got out of a car close to the street and brought him back to reality.

His sister told him to meet up with a woman. He was supposed to carry the doll around with him and if something happened, he should press the doll's belly. 'Press its belly?', he thought unbelievingly. He wanted to run away from a Mosque, why exactly should he believe in Brazilian voodoo?

He could feel the doll pulsing slightly in his hand. He blamed the cold for it. The wind got heavier, and some trees creaked loudly because of it. As he wanted to turn at a corner, he saw one of the three men on the pavement and knew immediately who he was. It was his uncle, together with two other men from the Mosque. He realized he was in danger and thought for a second about the direction he should go in.

Maybe they knew he was about to run away because he might have said something wrong himself. Despite the clues from his sister, he knew that he talked too much sometimes.

'Well. Press the belly.' He pressed the belly of the doll and realized there was a device hidden in it.

The eyes of the doll blinked in blue and white. He was relieved that it apparently was more than a voodoo doll, but he was still scared it couldn't do much in his current situation. He still had to go three blocks.

The place where he should meet this woman wasn't far from the Rhine and he thought in the worst case he would have to seek refuge in the water. Jumping in the water would probably still not as painful as getting his genitals crushed from three of his Mosque friends. The doll continued to vibrate, and his fingers started prickling already. He thought it must have been his heavily pulsating blood and he opened his hand but left it in his pocket.

His uncle called his name.

"Aca."

His legs trembled with fear once he heard his voice and he felt a lump in his throat. It was obvious this was a serious meeting so his heart beat faster and adrenalin flooded his body. The wind became heavier and Aca suddenly wanted to run. When he pulled out his hand of his pocket, the ugly doll seemed to grab his sleeve. The cheap invisible thread which held the glass beads together, was brittle and caught the fabric of his coat.

But then it fell to the ground and the knot at the end of its legs went lose and all the glass beads rolled away from him into different directions. Its bright eyes were still visible and the device in its belly didn't stop vibrating.

The wind caught the glass beads on the ground and spun them in the air. Aca was frozen and felt unable to just walk one more step. The men approached him. The two man who he didn't know the names of came from either sides and his uncle stood almost directly in front of him. One of them had a wooden club in his hand and the other one carried a bunch of ropes. The remains of the doll fell apart and the glass beads spun around, mixed up with the rain drops and created a statue of water. Aca's eyes were filled with dust and rain and he could only see the outlines of a woman who went up the street. The man with the club hit his hip and the pain soared up to his head, but he was unable to scream. To beat up a homosexual just to prove the own masculinity still seemed to be a sign of power for many men. Blood drenched Aca's trousers and the broken hip swelled up.

The woman who walked up the street became more visible and all four men were surprised when they saw a half-naked woman coming out of the storm. No one could say if this woman was out for a walk or if she approached them. However, everyone suddenly knew that she wasn't scared.

She was real and despite her determination, she didn't seem threatening. That's why the men from Mosque ignored her and continued with their holy task of hurting Aca. A kick hit Aca on his cheek and he fell to the ground.

From the other side at the beginning of the street and far away from the river, a small man came around the corner. He wore a purple hat. He almost looked like a pubertal boy at the age of around fifteen. Small and chubby. The men didn't see his face.

The flowing robes which covered the woman were of best quality and glowed despite the bad lighting. Apparently, she was naked and wet as the water shone on her tattooed skin. Her long hair graced her lovely curves from her head down to her knees. Her skin was covered with graceful tattoos.

The men from Mosque were surprised when she walked towards Aca and stopped right in front of him. Apparently, she had a plan. Aca laid on the ground and saw her face. He intuitively knew that she wasn't just a woman. He wanted to leave but his legs didn't obey.

One of the Mosque brothers approached the small man and told him to back off.

"Leave!", he said strictly.

But the man stopped for a moment and just continued to move more determined as if he forgot he was too small to face confrontations.

"Go away!", said the other Mosque brother in Turkish and the woman didn't react. She slowly moved towards the men and left Aca laying on the ground.

"Want something from me?!", gasped the other one out but he was barely intelligible.

"I want you." As soon as she finished this sentence, the whirl got stronger and a lasso caught the neck of one of the men. Her ropes fell to the ground and her body dissolved into a mixture of water and debris and a thunder filled the sky.

She achieved the desired effect with her nakedness and while the men were staring, Jenny used this opportunity.

Aca fainted, not knowing where the border to reality ended.

Everything happened within a few seconds and the men didn't find the courage nor the trust that they could withstand the fury which Jenny embodied.

The first man with the club acted quickly and hit the woman. He barely had time to think about if he did it because he was scared or because of an instinct of survival. Jenny's fingers pierced into his nose and shot a massive spurt of water up there. The water went through his throat into his lungs and he could only see a light at the end of the tunnel which he would never reach. No prayer, no God, just the pointless end of the violence in a life which was never fulfilled and very lonely. The other man dropped the bunch of ropes and the second men came to rescue him. But he was too late: His friend was already on the ground. He tried to kick the woman, but her body gave in. It looked like he kicked a puddle with his foot. A laugh accompanied the second thunder and the streetlights didn't seem to be able to shine through the darkness of the night. The woman's eyes became dark caves and her mouth turned into a devouring grimace. A dull scream came like a gurgle out of the throat of the desperate man. He was so scared; he fell to the ground. During the last moments of his life, he felt how the ropes, which he looked forward to using so much, whirled around his throat and pulled him up in the air. His eyes were frozen, and his mouth distorted unnaturally when he fell to the ground again.

Aca's uncle threw a knife at him to fulfil his holy task. However, he missed his target and only hurt Aca on his cheek. His uncle watched how the woman approached him and had barely time to finish his prayers when she started talking to him.

"I'm Jenny and Aca is now mine." Her index finger pointed challenging towards her chest and emphasized her female resistance in way, Aca's uncle would never underestimate a woman in his life, even though there weren't more than a few minutes left of it.

In the next morning, the police only found three beaten, dead bodies. The rain last night came and left so quickly; a lot of the street wasn't wet. Later on, the police reports stated that Aca's uncle was beaten up by two other man and stabbed in the end. The perpetrators were caught off guard by the storm and couldn't flee so they became victims of the water. There didn't seem the need for further investigations and everyone was happy to close the case without further work.

The police photographer captured the details of the crime scene and his last picture showed three bodies on the ground. He was tall and his black hair was tied back in a ponytail. Later on, they barely noticed that this photographer didn't belong to the police. If someone did notice it, they would have thought he was a reporter.

Aca disappeared and his family never looked for him. Only Sögun secretly thought about how this ugly glass-bead doll could have helped her brother.

Box of dolls

Almost two hours passed, and Richard already started thinking about dinner. The sun had already set behind the house and the balcony was in the shadows. He felt his legs getting colder and pulled the blanket from the balcony further up his thighs.

Richard felt dizzy and wanted to end this session. But his legs seemed heavier than usual and Eleonore finally managed to take a step forward.

"I don't feel very well, Leo. I'd rather stop here and continue tomorrow."

Eleonore got up and went to the edge of the balcony.

"Are you sure?"

Richard noticed a slight change in her behaviour, but he was already familiar with this. Patients with a behavioural disorder change their mood all the time.

"Wait for a moment." Eleonore went into her room and got her laptop.

"You have a computer in here?" She nodded and quickly put the dishes from the table to the floor and made space for her laptop.

"Yes."

This short break made Richard nervous because he knew that, despite how tired he was, Eleonore couldn't have that much fantasy and maybe those people from the agency were actually involved in this story.

"I'll tell you how I became what I am today. Crazy, instable and simply a mess sometimes." Eleonore's eyes seemed glassy and it was obvious that she was about to start to cry.

"Do you want to have a break?"

"No, Richard. I think I'm finally ready for the last part. The part I couldn't talk about until now."

Eleonore opened the laptop and turned it on. The noise of the humming hard drive accompanied Eleonore's story in the background.

"As you can see, there are posters on the walls of my room. Do you know this band?"

"No, Leo. I don't know much about the world of music."

He had a hard time smiling at her and he almost looked like a wax figure. The weather really bothered him apparently.

"Well, Richard, this band was called T-Weeds. They wanted to make heavy metal music and had very big dreams like many other bands where teenagers are involved in. I'll tell you the story of the singer of this group."

Richard nodded heavily and hoped the end of this story would come soon. He wanted to go home before it got dark.

"They were full of hope and already planned their world tour, but in the end, they didn't even get out of the city."

◆

"I'll go to the lake, aunty", whined a blonde girl. The girl obviously lied because she was already at the lake and it was a different one to the Starnberger lake where her aunty thought she was.

The shore of the river Loisach was a conservation area. For many years it was a popular destination for visitors from the whole of Bavaria. They went there with their families and friends to enjoy the views of the fresh-water beaches.

Like every summer, the forest grew thick and it smelled like rotten wood. On some beaches of the river were men and women who enjoyed their nudist beaches and wanted to soak in every ray of sunlight there was. There usually weren't any pubertal girls or boys around.

Reinhold, flatmate of Annabella, was only twenty-eight years old at this time and was happy because of the attentive eyes of the people who looked at his good-looking body.

On this day, Annabella brought a basket of snacks with her. Reinhold drove the old Renault and they chatted along about what they would do today after getting out of the car. He wasn't aware of the fact that almost everyone in his age looked good. If he did, he probably wouldn't have had that many beers when he was older. His bisexuality was just a creation of his fantasy as he never had sex with women before, but he still thought it was just a phase.

When they finally left the parking lot and entered the forest almost fifteen minutes later, they decided which beach they go to.

Reinhold played the keyboard and his heavy-metal band lacked opportunities to prove their skills. Another topic they talked about.

They talked for almost an hour about several topics until Annabella wanted to read vacancies and asked Reinhold to deal with the surrounding clients. Reinhold bathed his body in water and tried to get most of the attention of everyone by swimming and sunbathing.

After that, he left Annabella reading and went for a walk in the forest. Everyone who was familiar with the area knew, that every now and then there were other walkers who were looking forward to spontaneous pleasure. In Bavaria, a quickie in the woods is known just as well as in the other parts of the worlds, but no one talked about it. The fact that a lot of gay sex happened in the woods especially wouldn't be go-to topic at family dinners. Religious

Bavaria wouldn't ever think about, let alone talk about, topics like these.

It could be hard for men to appear discretely in the forests as their body could make it hard for them to act in discretion.

Despite his age, Reinhold didn't have a lot of experience and Annabella was a good friend, but he still hoped for his fairy-tale prince who would be interested in him. Everyone talked about those quickies in the woods. Sometimes, the stories weren't as nice as someone might have hoped but Reinhold still wanted to try his luck. Those were his first years in his own home, without his family. The last thing he wanted in his life, was to accidently start a family which would lead to the end of his independence. That was the reason why his relationships didn't last very long.

He went along a path and everyone he met gave him a feeling of depravity which demotivated him slightly. But he didn't want to give up. He was forced to walk in the shade because of his shyness, as well as the sunlight. There were nettles everywhere and he tried hard not to touch them. He was especially careful where he stepped as this region was known for its crossed vipers and their poison could get dangerous. However, it wasn't very likely to meet those shy, small animals anyways.

After he walked for more than one hour, his feet started hurting. He carried his clothes in his backpack and gave his body maximum liberty. He put down his towel on the ground under a tree and laid down naked, hoping unknown walkers wouldn't disturb his peace. He wanted to go back to Annabella but the desire to meet someone who came up to his expectations forced him to wait.

The Bavarian sun could be very aggressive and very stressful for white skin in just a short amount of time. That's why Reinhold got up after some time and went further into the direction of the mountains. He heard the trains for the tram and thought it was time to go home for him as well. He sent a text message to Annabella, hoping she would reply soon. He didn't expect to meet anyone special here anymore as all the good catches must have already left and his skin became quite sensitive here. His upper body was slightly sunburnt, and his face was red in some parts.

It was exhausting to walk up the mountains on a side path. Just fifty meters into the way he slipped and slit sideward, landing in a stinking heap. Moss and old leaves covered a lot of dry wood. Because of his sensitive skin, he suffered some injuries. Two twigs pierced his skin slightly.

He wanted to have a look at his injuries, but the smell was unbearable. It looked like the sun, which shone through the leaves, cooked a heap of excrements. He also smelled something sweet. Something raspberry and something banana. Reinhold had to think of the catalogue of the sommelier which he read recently. They wrote about a Point Noir with a chocolate scent with a hint of rubber tire. While he imagined how a sommelier would lick the asphalt to come to conclusions like these, Reinhold tried to free himself from all the twigs. As just kept on falling again, he felt his hand landing on a heap of sticky moss.

Somehow, he managed to roll to his side and get up. As he stretched, his eyes were fixed to the heap of moss. A bit of brown hair was decorated with some leaves and behind it was a motionless body.

He couldn't scream and running away wouldn't help as he had to orientate. He tried to pull himself together and to get his backpack back, which landed a few steps further away from him.

A woman, dressed in a see-through, white robe sat under a tree with her eyes wide open. Dirt and bits of the peaty ground covered her on some pars and Reinhold asked himself why she was here.

"Sorry", he said, like he had to apologize for being scared. That's when he realized she stared into space and looked confused.

He put on his jeans and tried to hide his panic. All his erotic thoughts vanished, and he didn't care about his looks anymore. For the first time, he was confronted with something that didn't fit in his protected life.

The woman mumbled something about a souterrain and the sun being too bright for her. He couldn't understand her properly and he wasn't sure if she actually said something that made sense.

He dropped a pin on his phone. Geolocation was very useful in situations like these, but it wasn't enough to stop his legs from trembling. He kneeled down and called Annabella. She didn't answer so he sent a text with his location and hoped she would try to find him,

He tried to look away from the smelling body of the woman, but he wouldn't be able to ban this image for the next few years. He called the police. But the police weren't synchronised to the modern world of computers yet. He had a hard time describing where he was, and they agreed on meeting at the parking lot of the tram. The police were very quickly but Annabella really wasn't. Reinhold still struggled with the shock and tried to lead the way to where Annabella already waited, despite his hiccups and sudden trembling.

He noticed he was still without his shirt and that the red patches on his skin were hurt by twigs and plants. A few ravens weren't happy about the sudden noises and the invasion into their forest. They didn't stop screaming.

Eventually they stopped and flew away. Reinhold was careful while he walked through the woods and tried to collect all his strength to be brave.

The two police officers were one man and one woman who was barely older than Annabella. She acted very professional as if this happened regularly. She didn't show her overextension at all. Time passed and the wind was cold.

The policewoman noted if the woman was conscious and if she could move. Although the woman had to be out here for several days, withstanding the cold and the weather, she got up quickly. She moved her lips, but no one could hear what she said. She stumbled slightly to the left and then to the right as if she was dancing. Reinhold didn't want to seem cold, but he wanted to go home as soon as possible, and Annabelle looked like she understood.

"Gazou", he heard the woman say.

The policeman accompanied both back to the parking space. He was very sympathetic and seemed to know what he had to do in situations like these. They could already hear the ambulance in the distance and some gazers stood close by.

"There's nothing of interest here!", shouted the police and waved to signalize that everyone should go to the side.

Annabella remembered the smell of the old woman and how she mumbled and laughed silently. The scent of a flower was noticeable between all those smells, even if it wasn't strong.

"Did she talk to you?", asked Reinhold as he saw Annabella's confused face.

"Yes." She seemed shocked as well and was looking for words. "But I think we should talk about this later."

Reinhold realized Annabella held a stuffed animal in her hands.

"Did the woman have this?"

"Yes, Reinhold. This is Gazou."

The policewoman was still busy getting the woman on the ambulance and her colleague could barely work because of all the gazers asking questions. And so, Annabella was left with an expression of shock on her face.

Two days later, the newspaper stated about the tragic discovery of Angelika Wiemer, former head of the Jane Andrew wellness hospital for women. Angelika, who got lost on the wet forest ways of Wolfratshausen, used to be a pretty girl, according to the old black and white picture. Mrs Wiemer looked like she was about forty years old on the picture which was actually much younger than she actually was. It looked like she was a completely different woman to who they found in the forest.

The fate of Mrs Wiemer remained a secret for Reinhold und Eleonore for the next two weeks.

A short article stated that Angelika Wiemer fled from the sanatorium. Unfortunately, the weather was too hard on her and she died after fighting for two further weeks on the intensive care unit. Her family invited Reinhold and Annabella to the funeral where they saw Angelika on a picture next to the coffin, which was decorated with white flowers. She seemed happy and very typical for women in the mountain regions of Bavaria. She had blonde highlights in the picture next to the coffin. This hairstyle must have been from a hairdresser in her earlier life as she didn't have any highlights when she was found in the woods.

She didn't have a big family. There were two elderly women. One of them was her mother and the other one must have been her sister. Reinhold thought they could've almost been twins. At the funeral was also Angelika's brother, who invited Reinhold and Annabella and four other men who didn't introduce themselves. However, two friends of Angelika's former, better life introduced themselves shortly. They were seated in the last row.

At the wake at the house of her parents, Reinhold got the opportunity to say his condolences. It was more of a way to handle the shock. He briefly talked to Angelika's friends who seemed very shocked.

There was a picture on top of the coffin showing the three of them at a protest on the lake.

He didn't remember much of this conversation, but one of the friends said, in between blowing her nose and crying, that she could've never imagined Angelika being in such bad conditions.

The officials didn't think an inspection was needed as Angelika seemingly lived in the hospital "Elysische Felder" and escaped despite her guard.

This hospital was the successor to her wellness hospital, which Angelika was the head of. Her husband and another doctor were the administration of it.

It was hard to walk on the wet street in Wolfrathshausen. It didn't explain how Angelika manged to get to here as the hospital is about thirty kilometres away, but there weren't many ticket controls on busses and trains in Munich, so no one was suspicious. Numerous bruises and cuts on her skin must have been down to twigs on bushes and trees and nothing else ever happened on this case.

Annabella brought Gazou and put him on her coffin.

"When I saw her in the foods, she briefly told me that there was a monster in her brain. I have to admit, it sounded slightly absurd. When I heard it, I realized she must have had fantasizing", said Annabella.

"I really don't want to make more out if this case then there is, but I'd love to hear more about her." Reinhold wasn't sure about this situation and it was his first funeral in his life. He didn't even go to the one of his own grandparents.

"I will talk to her guard and he will see me. I did kind of hear her last words, so I just want to follow up on this story to get a better understanding of it. There's something off with it. She must have been mentally ill as she was on medication."

"What do you mean?"

"She told me she wasn't crazy. She was on the run because the man who held her in the souterrain was a sadistic monster and also her husband. If I understood it correctly, she was held there for more than four years."

"Did you tell the police everything?"

"Yes. But they all seem to think that this woman really was crazy, and no one wants to make a real case out of it."

"Leave it, Annabella. We didn't know her, and we didn't have anything to do with her life."

"Just a quick conversation with her former guard and I will give up on this case."

"She broke her neck when the car crashed into the tree. The undertaker confirmed this as well."

The policewoman tried to talk as clearly as she could so Reinhold would finally stop arguing.

Reinhold observed that it seemed like the old, yellowed walls were renovated recently, but they left the old wallpaper on it, which wasn't in any better shape and it didn't smell too nice either.

"But they didn't know each other. What would Annabella want in this car? She has a car herself which she took to the hospital." Reinhold didn't agree again.

For a moment he got interrupted by another conversation of a police officer at the table next to them. He pulled himself back together and focused on the policewoman again.

"Yes. We know. But as Dr Simon explained after he woke up from the same accident, her car broke down. I checked it myself and the mechanic confirmed that one part of the car was too old which eventually led to a backfire. Dr Simon wanted to give Annabella Schumann a lift to the tram." The policewoman looked at him and felt sorry for Reinhold. She knew how confused he must've been. Reinhold thought about what he could say now but he didn't find any words. There was no point in further discussing it. Annabella died in a silly car crash.

"Her belongings are here until someone from her family picks them up. I'm sorry."

"I have a letter of authorization. "Reinhold handed her a folded piece of paper. She opened and read through it.

"That's fine. One last word from me, in case you need some kind of support, we have a social worker who you could talk to. He is specialized in traumata. It could be worth a shot, right?"

"I'm fine. I just can't understand how this happened. Annabella was so young. We have a band and a carrier and now everything is over." Tears shot into his eyes and the officer looked for a reason to leave the room quicker to avoid this emotional moment with him. It's always tragic when young people die, and she hated this part of her work.

Reinhold stayed for a few moments in this room by himself and finished the coffee which he got from a coffee machine. It was disgusting but it was the only thing that seemed real to him in this moment. The conversation of the other officers at the table next to him didn't seem to go as planned and everyone looked fuming. He listened to what they were saying without understanding anything. His conscience was foggy from the shock.

Annabella died because of a car accident on a country road on a late afternoon. A former guard of Mrs Wiemer was part of it. He fractured his legs during the accident and almost died. He found out it was too unfortunate as the person who caused the accident was on a motorcycle and he just drove away apparently.

Annabella's mother was in Morocco at a conference for Doctors Without Borders or something like this and Reinhold didn't know how to contact her. Her father died years ago, and Annabella didn't have many friends he knew except the other members of the band.

He was sure there was something off with the story the driver told them, but he naturally didn't trust anyone. That's why he shouldn't voice any accusations for which he didn't have any evidence.

He already put out an empty box for Annabella's stuff before he left his apartment.

He threw the bag with everything she had, which he got in a big envelope off of the police, into the box without even opening it.

In her last song, she wrote about people without faces. Annabella was very talented, and the style of her songs was similar to heavy metal in the sixties as her songs also had a lot of content. He put her last CD in the player and pressed play.

Obviously, what happened with Angelika Wiemer must have had an impact on her. If Reinhold could have imagined what happened, he had never asked for her help on this day.

Annabella was obsessed with what this woman experienced and used the information from their conversation in the forest for this song.

Reinhold listened to the lyrics and felt that Annabella wanted to convey more than just a song with them. Apparently, she wanted to tell about the mental torture Angelika had to go through. Very good content for an artist, Reinhold thought.

The lyrics almost sounded whiny and while he listened, he looked for her diary. Annabella used to write a lot of her experiences down to use them to compose lyrics for Reinhold's music.

When he finally found her pink diary, he also thought if he should rent her room out again. He knew, that, as soon as someone new moved in, he would suppress all of his memories with Annabella. He might even forget about her.

In this moment, he decided that, if the police couldn't help him, he would have to contact a friend of hers online so he could clarify this situation. He couldn't forget the suspicion Annabella had. The sun went down and he turned the light on to open the big envelope he got from the police.

The cloth bag with its Indian pattern which Annabella brought with her from India was folded up. There were a few traces of blood on it. There were other things women carry around like make-up, deodorant and a brooch in the form of a dragon fly as well.

He turned on his computer and opened the browser. He opened another tap and looked for Endhora.

Endhora was one of the alternatives for Anne's avatars who responded immediately.

Reinhold contacted Anne via her avatar as he tried to help a friend whose brother wanted to flee from Germany.

Her brother was Aca.

◆

"Yes, Richard. I have a lot in this house. Which, by the way, is mine since last year." For the first time, Eleonore spoke more confident and not as crazy as usually.

"What? It belongs to you?" It could be a manic fit if she actually believed this house belongs to her.

"Fashion, my dear, can bring you a lot of money and the payment of our employees and the rescue projects don't cost as much and we all know already that money isn't everything in life. Money won't buy us and we're not subject to consumption. Unbelievable, right?" Eleonore wasn't the same anymore and Paloma clearly wasn't just a lawyer. But those insights couldn't help Richard either.

Richard listened to the computer booting and Eleonore quickly raises a finger to signalize he should wait. Richard felt worse and wanted to protest.

"Listen to this", Eleonore suggested.

A girl sang a heavy-metal song and Eleonore turned the volume slightly up.

Richard seemed to know this song.

"Faceless Monks."

"Yes. I know this song."

"Annabella was the singer of this band. Annabella Greenleaves was her alias. She wrote this song when she realized the dead Mrs Wiemer was a victim. Anne will be here soon to confirm we researched properly and thoroughly. Paloma helped as well and took over your file from your attorney's office and found out everything we didn't have until then."

Memories came up and Richard realized he was in trouble. For the first time, crazy Eleonore seemed even more crazy.

Richard slowly started to sense that the dragon-fly brooch from the story of Annabella's accident could be the same one Eleonore was wearing right now.

"What is happening here?", asked Richard with even weaker voice.

In this moment, the door of the room opened. A tall woman entered, dressed like an American nurse out of films of the forties. She almost looked like a cartoon of a nurse, but her good taste and theatrical appearance couldn't be denied. It was the Honourable Sophie in one of her many costumes.

Richard recognized Mr Brenner's eyes and panic made his blood boil. He couldn't talk.

Richard also recognized Paloma as his employer.

"Richard." Eleonore got up and turned on her heels into his direction. He lowered her upper body dangerously into his direction. "Reinhold is a good boy, but he can't join the dots as well as I can. Or as well as Anne, our online expert. Do you understand?"

"It was an accident. I almost died as well." Richard pointed his open hands towards his injured legs. "What is happening here?"

"What happens is, my dear, that I will go to a place where laws don't apply, where lawyers manipulate the law." Paloma curtsied shyly. Eleonore laughed because of the joke and they could hear a creepy laugh from under Paloma's hair which she always wore brushed down over her face.

'Are those women crazy? What did they plan?'. Asked Richard himself in his mind. He was barely able to speak.

Richard felt dizzy because of the sedatives they gave him. He was scared and his heart was beating heavily in his chest.

"Are the sedatives effective yet?", asked Paloma as if she'd just ignore Richard being there.

"Apparently, you're ten minutes too early. You told me it'd unfold within four sessions", said Eleonore, almost as if she was complaining.

"You can't say it for sure. Sometimes it works faster and others take longer."

"What are you talking about?" There was spit running out of his mouth. Richard lifted his hand to wipe it away, but he didn't seem to be strong enough and his hand just fell down again. "That's against the law", he added slightly sullenly.

"Well, my dear. I will now tell you one last story or a singer. A young and innocent singer who just wanted to help an old woman who was looking for justice during the last minutes of her life."

"I'm sorry Richard but being here is not the same as to defend you in court as your lawyer." Paloma smiled under her hair which covered the left side of her face.

Richard's eyes were rigid because of how scared he was. He recognized something in this scenario, but it was too late.

"Six years ago, you were a psychologist and together with your friend Herbert, you came up with an idea. You locked up Angelika Wiemer, Herbert's wife, and declared her as mentally instable. By the way, our poison is better than what you gave Angelika back then."

"It only needs to be administered four times and can be put in tea instead of juice as well." Honourable Sophie sounded like an advertisement for mediation on TV.

Eleonore looked him deep in the eyes. That was the moment when Richard realized how angry she was and how dangerous his situation could be.

"The dragon-fly brooch seemed familiar to you, am I right?" Eleonore paused for a moment and waited for Richard to react.

His eyes were glassy, and he seemed sleepy.

"One song and a brooch are everything that remains of a smart girl and a woman called Mrs Wiemer who left behind a story about a basement with scratched walls."

"An accident", protested Richard feebly.

"Yes. That's what I thought as well. You wanted to kill yourself when Annabella confronted you with the realization, she had in the forest. Must have been fate, right?"

An avenger or a crazy woman. Richard couldn't decide and it didn't help that she was accompanied by two other people who looked even more frightening: a woman who covered half her face under her hair and a crazy drag.

"Herbert is waiting for you and I'm sure we'll look after you two just fine." Sophie unfolded a wheelchair and heaved Richard into it.

"Gutto looked after Herbert. A tragic accident", said Paloma with a sad look on her face. "Herbert cut with the chainsaw you could hear trough the cable and suffered an electric shock. He's in a coma now."

"If it didn't work today as well, I should've improvised with something. You have to mix your drinks better", moaned Eleonore.

"Don't kill the joy. Anne caught everything on her computer through the camera of your unicorn brooch which she handed out to you. The service here is of best quality. You simply complain too much."

Sophie cleaned Richard's lips with a paper towel.

Everyone laughed except Richard who felt convulsions running through his body. Those convulsions were the last thing he felt until his body was put on a bed in the basement.

Next to him as another freshly made bed and Herbert was on it.

◆

Reinhold sat on his computer and read about the horrible accident at the hospital 'Elysische Felder'.

Angelia Wiemer's husband suffered an accident with his chainsaw while he was working in the garden. He must have been in shock because his wife died so suddenly. The property was bought by an anonymous aristocrat.

A chat window popped open and Anne texted him under her alias Endhora.

'Did you read about the horrible things which happened at the hospital?'

'No', she lied.

'I thought nothing what happened but as you texted me, I should believe in karma, I thought you must be an esoteric now.'

'I only believe in justice and if they really did something, the universe would handle it. What happened?'

Reinhold was so excited; his fingers couldn't type properly.

'A chainsaw accidentally cut through the power able and the doctor of the hospital gave him the wrong medication for his diabetes. The police think it was an accident.'

Reinhold sent a sticker of a man hitting his head on the table.

'Bad luck.'

Anne sent an emoticon of a meditation unicorn.

A short break indicated Reinhold was typing.

'You don't have anything to do with it, right?'

'I wish. I'm too phlegmatic for things like these but I made sure the family will think well about Angelika Wiemer.'

'How did you do that?'

He sent a shocked emoji with hands around his screaming face.

'The shock which she had to go through and the link to the stuffed animal Gazou were tragic and something that needed to be solved.'

Anne sent a link to a newspaper article. It stated about a girl who was mistreated years before and was saved by a woman with ginger hair. This woman received Gazou as a present. The perpetrator was described by the girl as a man without a face.

The girl stated in an interview with a reporter that she went on holidays in Bavaria. The following should've happened years ago in this region.

She and a girl played at a river when a man she couldn't describe, approached them and took her with him. He forced her to the ground, and she thought she must die now. She described these moments of fear so well, you could feel it while reading the article.

When the perpetrator wanted to abuse her sexually, a woman approached and fought the man. She didn't know if there was a fight of if the woman killed the man, but he disappeared.

As a sign of gratitude, the woman received a stuffed animal with the name Gazou.

She didn't think about this incident and tried to forget about what happened. She was thankful to finally see this woman again and, although it was only after she died, she thanked Angelika's family for her brave commitment.

Reinhold read the article and replied with *'Thank you.'* It wasn't long until he received a report saying:

'Unknown user or profile deleted by the system.'

Appendix

The model agency "The Valley" was a concept which I developed twenty-two years ago at an exhibition in Munich.

There were six people dressed in diva clothes in bombastic colours. Something of pink flamingo and a bit of the famous Bai Ling.

Since then, I stared creating different femmes' fatales or other scurrile characters like the Honourable Sophie.

As a comic enthusiast myself, I designed my novels, so the characters crossed their ways again every now and then, like in other groups of heroes. Some stories are about solo-appearances like in the books "Paloma" or "The Muse".

I hope I can make my readers happy with a few other upcoming stories.

Many situations I write about in my novels are based on regional events and partly on my own actions as a protester against animal cruelty or for environmental protection. But I want to reassure to all my readers that I don't have technical skills like Gutto, nor do I adopt measures as harsh as Jenny.

Everything that happens is just karma.

Further publications of the author

German Novels
- Altreia, Drama, 1998
- Geheimnis der verdorrten Rosen, Mystery, 2009 – Reimo Verlag *
- Virtuelle Liebe, Kurzroman, Thriller, 2016 *
- Paloma, Kurzroman, Thriller, 2016 *
- Die Muse, Kurzroman, Erzählung, 2016 *
- Post Mortem Kino, Roman, Drama, 2016 *
- Die Heilerin, Roman, Thriller, 2017 *
- Geheimnis der verdorrten Rosen, Mystery, 2017 (neue Version) *
- Das Zauberspiegel des Eros, Roman, Thriller, 2017 *
- Das Tal, Roman, Thriller, 2017 *
- Jahreszeiten der Sünde, Roman, Thriller, 2018 *
- Die blutige Soiree des Grafen Rasnov, Krimi, 2018 *

German Graphic Novels
- Virtuelle Liebe, 2018 *
- Paloma, 2018 *
- Die Muse, 2019 *

English Novels

- Virtual Affairs, 2018 *
- The Muse, 2018 *
- The Muse – Graphic Novel, 2018 *

German audio books

- Virtuelle Liebe, 2018
- Paloma, 2018
- Die Muse, 2018

Art catalogue

- Geliebter Vater, 1995 *
- The new Artist, 1996 und 1997
- Liebe in Stücken, 2009 *
- Kunstkatalog, 2010
- Liebe in Stücken, Edition II, 2016 *
- Kunstkatalog, 2017 *
- Kunstkatalog, 2018 *
- Kunstkatalog, 2019 *

(*) Listed in the German National Library